SINNER

SINNER

THE DEADLY SEVEN, ORIGINS

LANA PECHERCZYK

www.lanapecherczyk.com

When we save our children, we save ourselves.

ONE

FLINT

FLINT FYDLER KEPT his head down, hat low and bag close to his body as he walked into the lobby of Biolum Industries, late for the second time that week. He swiped his ID at the turnstile and pushed through. It wasn't as though he was hiding something. He just knew what came next. Every damn time.

A black uniformed security guard sized him up. The dude must bench twice his weight, and his neck was as thick as Flint's thigh. A revolver was strapped under his right arm. A Taser hung from his belt. With a wary flicker behind the guard's eyes, and a twitchy trigger finger, Flint knew if he sneezed the wrong way, the man would take him down. Ex-Marine. Had to be. Just like his buddies upstairs in front of the Project room.

The guard stopped Flint with a sturdy palm to his chest. Flint glared at the intrusion and bit his lip to halt the scathing comment on the tip of his tongue. He wasn't sure what the big guy had against him. Could be his Dodgers baseball cap, his level five clearance, or maybe the fact that Flint had a beard when the brute couldn't grow a 'stache.

Like every other morning, Flint swallowed his words. He knew when to pick his battles, and this wasn't one.

"You," growled the guard. "Spot bag scan."

"Dude, really?" Flint slipped his satchel off his shoulder and put it on the conveyor. "You see me every day."

The man grunted, opened Flint's bag and checked inside.

Just what he needed after the morning he'd had. First, the flat on the way to work, then the bald spare, and finally the state of his anemic bank account making the purchase of a new tire impossible. He ended up jogging to work when he'd already been on a ten-mile run. His quads were killing him.

"Fucktard," Flint mumbled.

"What did you say?" the guard asked.

"I said custard. Watch out for the custard." Flint pointed to the small tub of pudding in his bag.

"Right." The guard lifted a dubious eyebrow and then shoved the bag down a conveyor track to the X-ray machine where an attendant watched from a seat on the other side.

Flint winced as his bag rattled. "Careful. I got priceless tech in there."

"Don't care. Move to the side, and wait for the scan results."

Flint shook his head defiantly. "I created that scanner. If I wanted to, I could beat it. You know that, right?"

The dude narrowed his eyes. "Spot bomb scan. Lift your arms up."

"I don't have time for this. Jesus *fucking* Christ."

He heard a feminine gasp behind him and whirled to face everything wrong with the world. Slick black hair in a ponytail. Luscious lips, a rosy little nose, and, fuck it, big brown eyes that belonged on Miss America Latina. A stunning contradiction because any woman whose hips filled out pants *that* way had no business being a nun. Her crisp white shirt was supposed to be modest, but her breasts pushed at the woolen vest, drawing it tight. A modern nun and walking sin, Sister Mary Margaret made his heart go bump and his words fail, because every time he saw her, ah jeez... off limits.

Flint's neck itched as Sister Mary stared back, big doe-eyes blinking. Caught. She caught him. Heat flamed his cheeks, and that just made him shittier. But the Sister and he went way back. Two years of charged banter, unfulfilled sexual tension, and love-hate bickering. She could take whatever he dished out.

"The fuck you staring at?" he said with a smile twitching his lip.

The little minx blinked at Flint, feigning innocence for

their spectators. As if she didn't gasp to play into her stereotype. She fluttered her lashes. "Who, me?"

"You heard me."

"Hey," the guard snapped at Flint. "Respect."

Flint almost snapped back, but was held captive by the Sister's eyebrow lifting—gearing up.

Come on, Flint thought. *Show me some of that fiery Latino spirit.* It was just the thing he needed to brighten his morning.

She folded her arms under her breasts, pushing them up. A hip cocked and then she gave him a scathing once over. Flint could smell the coconut in her hair. He was about to get a preachy tongue lashing, he knew it. He loved it. He wanted it. He squeezed his eyes shut and prayed.

He heard a shuffle as she stepped closer. She whispered near his ear, hot breath tickling his skin, "I'm not sure what I'm staring at. They haven't labeled it yet."

Flint's gaze snapped open. Their cheeks were inches apart. She smiled, full lips stretching to light up her face. A husky laugh and a flirty wink escaped her.

Instant hard-on.

Fuck he was going to hell, and he wanted more. But pushing her was dancing with danger. He had his demons, and she had her vows.

"Apologies for the disrespect, ma'am," the guard said, breaking their moment. "You go on through."

"Thank you," Sister Mary replied and pulled aside

from Flint, her smirk still there. "Peace be with you. Both of you."

The two men watched her walk away, hips swaying.

Something whispered at Flint's feet and he looked down. A white envelope had landed on his boot. Must have fallen from her pocket. He bent to retrieve it, collected his bag from the conveyor and jogged to catch up with her as she entered the elevator bound for his floor.

TWO

MARY

MARY SMILED as she entered the elevator and punched level sixteen. The cute tech-genius who worked on her floor always made her smile. She wasn't sure whether it was his blustering and cursing, his passion for his inventions, or the way his beard and hair was trimmed to perfection as he leaned over a neatly arranged desk of nuts, bolts and computer chips. He also left secret treats labeled with her name in the break room fridge. Last week she got a Baci chocolate. The week before, a Krispy Kreme donut. She wondered if he'd put anything in today.

The truth was that any chance they had to share the same air lifted her spirits even if they spent most of the time trading insults and witticisms. For the five minutes and twenty-five seconds it took to brew her cappuccino, and him to stir his long black, they were alone.

For the past two years, Flint Fydler had wiggled his

way into her thoughts daily. Her ten a.m. sojourn to the break room was the highlight of her week.

Just yesterday, they'd spent the entire break trading opinions on the escapades of the country's new President. Mary had simply mentioned that a female President would never have been caught dead dipping her wick into her intern, and Flint replied that a female can't because she doesn't physically have a wick to dip. Mary's resulting argument for the case of feminist dipping had been both sensually empowering and exhilarating. She loved to shock him with her entirely non-nunlike vocabulary. Of course, she wouldn't dream of acting like that in front of anyone else.

But she trusted him.

The thought slammed into her.

She trusted a *man*.

As absurd as it sounded for a member of the Hildegard Sisterhood to trust a man, she knew that above all else in her life, he'd always keep her secrets safe.

Pretending to be a nun was stifling. Looking after the children in the Project room was something she hadn't expected. Rewarding, eye-opening, and a change in perspective. Nobody except the head scientist Gloria knew Mary's secret identity, but with Flint, she didn't have to fully pretend. She could let her personality out to play.

Maybe she wanted to be caught out. Maybe she wanted *him* to catch her.

Except, she had a heavy burden to carry.

It was this burden that urged her to hit the "close"

button on the elevator, even when she caught sight of Flint's lithe body jogging toward her. The doors started closing, and she relaxed enough to feel a pull in her aching back. She rolled her shoulders to ease the pain. Her workout this morning had been brutal, and she had only herself to blame. The rigorous hour-long daily routine was of her own making, but she had no choice. It was almost time. She had to be strong. She had to be ready. The growing sense of dread coating her insides reminded her of that, and the last thing she needed was a distraction in the shape of a tall, sexy man. Not when the Sisterhood's secret plan was so close to fruition.

A large hand slotted between the closing elevator doors, and Mary jolted. A boot wedged in at the bottom. Flint's large body began squeezing through the tiny crack.

He wasn't going to make it.

"Shit. Fuck. Hold the door," came his deep male voice.

Mary considered hitting the "open" button. That's what a nun would do. But it was too much fun watching him squirm. Within seconds, Flint punched through in a burst and knocked her against the wall. His brandy brown eyes looked apologetic until he realized his baseball cap had left his head and was caught in the door. It slowly moved down the join as the elevator moved. He grasped, crouched and tugged.

The muscles in Flint's back rolled and bunched through his T-shirt. Mary allowed herself a moment of visual stimulation as he put his weight into one final tug that set his cap free.

He straightened and quickly smoothed his hair, replacing his hat—backward—then caught her gaze. His light irises were rimmed in dark brown. The same dark brown as his hair and beard. Having spent most of her life under the tuition of feminist nuns, she hadn't fully appreciated the joy of a well groomed man. Until now. The razor sharp line of his facial hair accentuated his strong jawline, and Mary knew, without a doubt, that he spent countless hours a week dedicated to his presentation. He struck her as the type who set his mind to something with dogged determination.

His straight brows snapped together.

"I know you heard me," he said.

"I'm sorry?"

"I asked you to hold the door."

Mary stifled her amusement. "I'm sure I don't know what you're talking about."

"Cut the bullshit, Sister. You act all pious around everyone else, but I'm onto you."

Mary's heart leapt into her throat and, for a split second, she feared their unspoken rule was about to be broken. She should've kept her snarky retort to herself, but he'd made it so easy. Her bottom lip dragged between her teeth, and the urge to wipe that smug smile off his face won. "If anyone is getting onto anyone around here, it'd be me."

That came out wrong.

He stepped closer and the walls of the lift closed in. Mary hadn't realized she'd backed up until her butt hit the wall and he placed a hand on the space beside her head, lips perilously close to hers. *Sweet Mother* he smelled delectable. Musky, manly and with a touch of mint.

"You're no nun," he said, voice low and intimate. "Admit it."

Her breath hitched. He was so close to the truth.

She pushed his chest with a flat hand but he didn't budge. A well-aimed jab to the carotid would drop him, but she couldn't remove her palm from his chest, or tear her gaze from his.

Electricity zipped through her as he lifted his free hand to cover hers.

Stop me if you dare, his dark eyes challenged, eyebrow arching confidently.

Her own arched back. *I dare.*

Slowly, painfully, gloriously, he slid their joined hands down the hard slabs of his chest. Her fingers rippled over his ribs, then his abs. Down. Down. Desire bloomed in her belly, pooling low and, heaven forbid, she wanted to explore further, but... *mission first.*

She snatched her hand back, and he released a throaty laugh.

What cheek! What nerve. For all he knew she was a bona fide nun. It was one thing for her to flirt, but it was another to physically cross the line. "You are... the rudest...

most—" She blinked, unable to get the words past the lump in her throat.

"Lost for words, Sister?" He kissed the air. "Most what? C'mon, tell me what you really think. Let's stop our secret dance."

She flattened her lips.

"No?" he added with a snort. "You want to be a nun as much as I want to be a ballerina."

"You're insane."

"No, I'm perceptive. The other nuns don't even know I'm alive, but you... you give me those sultry bedroom eyes, and that mouth full of sass, and I go hard. Every damn time."

Her eyes widened.

"Admit it, Sister. You like getting me hot and bothered, don't you? It gives you some sort of sick pleasure to arouse a man who can never have you... unless..." He rubbed his beard, contemplating. "Rethinking your calling? Is it my devastating good looks? My charm? My beard?"

"Your massive ego? Sure. Sure it is. Ugh. You genius types are all the same." Her words came out, but her mind was stuck on the fact he'd said he got hard when she looked at him.

He smirked. "So it's my mind."

"It's none of your business, that's what it is. If you think you know the first thing about me, you're sorely mistaken." She couldn't believe it. Things had never gone this far between them. Never escalated to physical, but always stayed verbal. It was just the kind of wake-up call she needed.

"C'mon, Sister. Give me something. This tension is killing me." He frowned as he dipped his head, all playfulness gone. "I'm tired of this no-man's-land we live in. I want more." When she didn't reply, he pulled away. "Okay. Whatever. Be a nun. Don't be a nun. Act sexually frustrated around me, act pious around them. I don't really give a shit. I got my own issues."

He adjusted his satchel over his shoulder and turned to face the front.

"That you do," she said, and hit the button for her floor again.

God, she hated her job sometimes. Why couldn't she have been born normal, without psychic powers? Why couldn't she meet boys, make love for days at a time, and worry about the world later? Why was this lift so goddamned slow?

A long shuddering sigh escaped her. Perhaps she should have added something about him doing penance, but she wasn't quite sure of the rules. Her time as a Sisterhood novitiate was filled with combat training rather than praying for forgiveness.

The silence stretched as they watched the light climb through the numbers. Mary could almost feel Flint's urge to speak, and when he opened his mouth and shut it again, she wasn't surprised. She didn't need a vision to know he wasn't finished with her.

Her prophetic visions had ripped her from an idyllic childhood in Mexico. She remembered the moment her mother turned on her with a burning clarity. Mary had been at a family gathering to celebrate her grandfather's birthday. Crowded into the clay brick courtyard for the festivities, she'd felt faint. So much noise. So many smells. The mouth watering spices. The cheerful dancing and music. But the heat she had felt rise in her body that day wasn't from the sun. The sharp needles that stabbed behind her eyes signaled the onset of a vision. Her first. She'd fainted dead on the floor, and when she had come to, she couldn't help crying in anguish that her grandfather was about to die. She'd pointed at him, whimpering, "El abuelo morirá." *Grandfather will die.*

Initially, her mother laughed and joked. "Not yet, *Mija*. Not yet."

But within the hour, her grandfather had suffered a heart attack.

She was infamous overnight. *Bruja*, they called her. *Witch.*

They thought she'd cursed him.

But her father figured out she could predict the future. They took her from psychic circuit to psychic festival. Round and round the country they went. She had only been ten years old, yet she remembered like yesterday. She had no friends as they were always moving about, and the costumes her parents made her wear did little to make her fit in. All the money she made went to them while she was left to scrounge in the trash for food.

There was one good thing her gift gave her, it put her in the path of the Hildegard Sisterhood and gave her the resources to be a part of something bigger. The Sisterhood's secret mission to promote the rise of women to power instead of a corrupt male government couldn't exactly come to fruition with a bunch of innocent God-fearing women. No. She was the Sisterhood's dirty little sinner, their necessary evil, and she had a higher calling than raising the Project children.

Society was crumbling around them. Every day crime worsened and women feared to walk in their neighborhoods alone for fear of assault. How could they establish a female leader to unite the world when sin was tearing it down?

Then Mary's visions had alerted the Sisterhood to the science experiment within the walls of Biolum Industries. The Vatican, government defense contractors, and unnamed silent partners bankrolled the joint venture, and the Sisterhood made it their business to volunteer nuns to raise the test-tube children who were created to fight sin with sin.

Two scenarios had played out in Mary's prophecies. One where the children were molded into being the world's saviors, and one where they were its destruction. Mary was the Sisterhood's failsafe. If they couldn't influence the children, then... no one would.

Today, for the first time in two years, Mary had doubts.

Suddenly, sharp needles stabbed behind her eyes. Panic gripped her heart and squeezed. *Not now. Not here. Oh please, Lord. Not now.* The warning of pain gave her just enough time to slam the emergency stop button on the elevator.

She spun to Flint, agony making her woozy. "Don't call anyone. Please. I just need a moment."

"Mary?" He held his hand out to her.

"Promise. You won't..." The words died on her lips as she reached for him and darkness swallowed her whole.

THREE

FLINT

THE ELEVATOR JERKED to a halt and Sister Mary Margaret collapsed.

Holy shit. Holy *goddamned* shit. Flint raced to catch her, but she slipped through his arms and they both tumbled to the floor.

She was out.

He slipped his palm beneath her head and lifted it from the hard floor onto his lap.

He swallowed. "Sister, are you okay?"

Not a murmur. Only soft, shallow breathing.

He touched her cheek gently with the back of his hand.

Soft. Hot. Was it hot? He didn't know.

Shit. Not good.

Crackles came through the speaker on the instrument panel, and then a male voice spoke. "Everything okay in there?"

Flint weighed a response in his mind. She said not to call anyone. That she just needed a moment. His mind whirled, caught between the desire to honor her wishes, and the urge to protect her. But... a nun telling him not to call anyone. It didn't feel quite right. Maybe she was having a stroke, or an aneurism, and it confused her. Or maybe she was diabetic. He had that pudding in his bag. He was going to give it to her anyway, may as well do it now.

It could also be an epileptic fit; the silent kind.

He'd heard sometimes epileptics didn't like a fuss. They knew they'd be okay in a few minutes and hated the paramedics coming. Epilepsy. That must be what it was. Surely.

Thinking back, though, she didn't look confused when she'd begged him with those big round eyes. *Please*, she'd said, all sass and wickedness gone. His chest constricted.

"Hello?" came the voice on the speaker, this time with more urgency. "Please respond." Then, when he didn't reply: "Press the red button on the panel to speak. Hello? I can see you. I know you're there."

Flint glanced up and noted the camera in the corner.

Mary murmured at that point, a crease etched between her brows. Maybe she'd be okay. He would keep her head from touching the ground. The tension in his shoulders eased a little more when she sighed, and it was a glorious sight. The color returned to her cheeks. She squirmed in a way that made him think of things he shouldn't be thinking. And she was on his lap. And he was going to hell.

"If you don't respond, we will send a technician down and pry the doors open."

Flint didn't answer.

Sister Mary's eyes popped open and air wheezed into her lungs.

"My goodness," she croaked. "I have to tell them. I have to warn them."

"Tell who?" Flint asked.

"It's happening."

"What's happening? Sister, are you okay?" Maybe she'd hit her head.

Her black pupils dilated and contracted as she focused on his face and then noticed him. Her hands fluttered to where his hands cradled her head. "Flint."

She said his name. Jeez he liked that.

"Are you okay? You kind of... fainted."

"Did anyone see? Have you told anyone?"

"No, I haven't... unless"—he glanced up at the roof—"the camera saw, but they can't hear."

"Shoot." She followed his glance up to the camera. "Shoot, shoot, shoot."

She rolled off him and snapped to her feet in a well-balanced move that confounded him. A minute ago, she was fainted on the floor, now she was the picture of perfect health. Better, in fact. She appeared determined, strong, and ready.

"Is there a problem with the cameras?" he asked.

Sister Mary's focus narrowed on him.

"Look," Flint continued, "I won't say anything. You can trust me, Sister. You once told me that you were given up by your parents. That you were an orphan. I know trust must be hard to come by, but I'm telling you the truth. I won't say anything."

She frowned. "When did I say that?"

"A few months ago, during one of our coffee breaks, I was telling you how my mother was giving me a hard time about—I can't even remember—but you said the fact that she wants me in her life is a good start and you mentioned you weren't wanted by yours. Are you embarrassed about having epilepsy?"

"Yes. That's it. Epilepsy. It's a condition Biolum Industries won't look favorably on, and—"

Flint held up his hand. "Say no more. I got your back."

"You have my back?"

"Yeah sure, I mean, I won't tell anyone and... if you want, I could"—he leaned in to whisper—"wipe the camera footage so no one knows."

"You can do that?" Her tone sounded like no one had ever done something nice for her before.

"Yeah, sure, give me a computer and a screwdriver and I can do almost anything."

A broad grin split her face, transforming her features into pure perfection. She let out a sigh of relief and then hit the emergency button on the wall with her fist. "Great. I would really appreciate that, thank you."

Flint nodded, but his mind caught on the way she'd

punched that button. Confident, well aimed... she wasn't even looking. Maybe this was why he allowed himself to feel the way he did when around her; she acted nothing like a nun. But, then again, he knew jack about them and he was probably projecting what he wanted to believe. He had to stop torturing himself.

As the elevator arrived at the top level of the building, the Sister turned to him and placed a gentle hand on his arm. She tipped up on her toes and kissed him on the cheek, lingering longer than socially acceptable. Electricity zinged from her lips down to curl his toes.

"Thank you, Flint. I don't know what I would've done without you." She blushed. "Maybe you were right about us. Just a little."

The door pinged open, and she left.

Well, shit. That was definitely not imagined. That was flirt.

He held the door open. "So... coffee at ten?"

She sent a cryptic smile over her shoulder.

"So, that's a yes?" he asked.

Sister Mary Margaret kept walking toward reception.

Flint stood there, frozen, until the elevator doors started closing again. Remembering the camera and his promise, he raced toward his work area, whizzing past reception without another thought. He didn't stop by Barry's lab bench where body parts and weird animals grew in large glass cylinders, and he raced past the genetics lab full of test tubes and Petri dishes. Finally, he pushed into the workshop area where drills whirred and soldering irons sizzled, leaving an acrid fragrance in the air. His workstation was the furthest from the entrance. Nothing behind him but the window and a devastating drop to the city floor below. Perfect.

It wasn't until he placed his satchel bag on his work desk that he wondered, why the fuck would a nun be afraid of someone discovering her epileptic fit?

FOUR

MARY

MARY CALMLY WALKED past reception where Lizzy smiled widely from her desk. Brown haired and impeccably presented, Lizzy had a mind like a vice. Her smile may have seemed innocent enough, but she was the Project's first gatekeeper. If she didn't recognize a face, a silent alarm would be tripped, and security personnel would sweep into the room to remove the threat for further questioning.

Mary nodded at Lizzy and continued down the east corridor to the Project room. When she was out of sight, she stopped and leaned against the cold wall. The temperature anchored her and gave her a moment to gather her senses. What had happened in the lift with Flint... Her eyes closed and she inhaled, attempting to wash the feel of him away. It wasn't the brazen flirting, or the physical crossing of the line—that run of their joined hands down his front—it was the way he'd instantly rallied to her aid.

I got your back.

She was ashamed she'd flirted with him, but she needed that footage erased. Better one person be suspicious of her than many. Especially now. Flint was tangled in this as much as she was, she'd *seen* it in her recent vision.

Mary exhaled slowly. To remind herself of her mission, she went to retrieve her latest coded letter from the Sisterhood, but found it missing from her pocket. Only the pebble she'd picked up on her morning walk was there. Sweat prickled her scalp.

Was it a sign?

A missing communication from the Sisterhood, but the presence of a gift she intended for Flint.

The letter had given her the green light to extract the children, and failing that, eliminate them. The thought left her hollow inside, but the burden was her purpose and she alone had trained for it. Sacrifice a few lives to save billions. The future she'd envisioned if they turned bad gave her night terrors. But if there was a chance they could be good...

For the first time in years, Mary doubted her orders. Didn't everyone deserve a chance to come back from evil?

Flint didn't seem the type of man who would condone the Sisterhood's mission. He didn't even know the kids existed. He probably thought he was working for some great humanitarian project like most other employees. During their coffee breaks, he'd always gone on about how good it felt to be doing something right for the world. He'd be devastated if he knew the truth—that they were building human weapons of mass destruction.

With a start, Mary realized she cared what Flint thought of her, and she *never* cared what anyone thought.

She shook her head. Two years caring for children had made her soft. It didn't matter if the letter went missing. It wasn't a sign her plan was doomed. It was a simple mistake. Now wasn't the time to have second thoughts.

Mary continued down the hall and around the corner to a second corridor. This one ended with a heavily guarded door. Like the men in the lobby downstairs, these wore protective clothing. Unlike the men downstairs, these carried assault rifles and tracked her arrival until she flashed her ID in their faces.

"Morning, boys."

"Morning, Sister."

"Another quiet day at the office?"

They smirked.

"Another quiet day in—say, what was it you did in there again?" The dark-skinned man who spoke had "M.Redmond" on his name badge. Redmond was brown-skinned, in his forties, and muscled like a bodybuilder.

"Nice try," Mary replied. "You know I've signed an NDA."

"We have ways of making you spill your secrets," teased the tattooed one with his sleeves rolled up. His name badge said "J.Preedy." Preedy looked to be mid-thirties, had short dark hair, and a scar gouging his cheekbone. That kind of marking only came from stupidity, or ruthlessness. She placed her bets on the latter.

"I'd like to see you try," she countered.

The men laughed, but Mary didn't because she knew she could take them despite their military training.

"Good answer," Redmond said.

Mary's gaze flicked to his tattoo, same as Preedy's. "That's from the Marines, isn't it?"

"Yes, ma'am. Means always loyal."

"This is a far cry from a war zone. So who are you loyal to now?"

"Whoever is writing the check."

Mary smiled. Good. Perhaps they could be bribed if necessary. If not, she'd been graced with ten years hard training in the Art of Warfare around the world, including a stint with the Marines. There wasn't a person alive she couldn't take down.

Being the Sisterhood's Sinner would do that to you.

The past two years spent at Biolum Industries weren't her first in the field. Before that, she'd been deployed by the Sisterhood around the world, silently infiltrating male dominated government departments and powerful house-holds. Each time she'd successfully manipulated her way inside, pretending to be someone she was not. Sometimes a nun, sometimes a seductress, but always lethal.

Satisfied with her ID, Redmond stepped aside and indi-cated to the retinal scanner embedded in the wall. Mary held her eyes to the plate. In seconds, the solid white door clicked open, revealing the distant sound of a crying baby. Her insides clenched. The child must be distressed if Mary could hear her wail through the solid double paned plate-glass that separated the children from the lab.

When Mary stepped into the lab, she took a moment to assess. Two scientists sat making notes on computers and testing samples of bio-hazardous material collected from the children. Beyond the two-way mirror were the living quarters of seven children, soon to be eight. Beds, cots, play mats, tables, a bathroom, a kitchenette, and an electronic doorway to a tiny rooftop garden with high walls to block the view of the city below. In the middle of the quarters, Sister Magdalene bounced a red-faced and tearful one-year-old in her arms.

"Good. You're here," Mary said to Gloria as she studied a microscope.

Gloria didn't lift her head, but the second scientist Mao, faced Mary and put his finger to his lips in a "shush" sign.

It was common knowledge not to interrupt Gloria deep in process. The genius genetic-engineer had her quirks, that was for sure. The company pandered to every one of them because the success of the Project depended on what was in her head. And if someone triggered a meltdown by not respecting her process, what was in her head stayed in her head.

There was no time for waiting.

Mary cleared her throat then hummed a tune familiar

to Gloria. It was a trigger they'd both agreed on if ever Mary had to disrupt the status quo and change the plan. Within seconds, Gloria lifted her gaze from her scope and locked eyes onto Mary.

A classically beautiful woman, Gloria had long, dark lustrous hair like Mary's own, but the similarities ended there. Gloria's hair was wavy and pulled back in a disregarded top knot. She was a pale, blue-eyed delicate wildflower where Mary was an olive skinned, dark-eyed piece of machinery programed for one lethal purpose—to enforce the Sisterhood's mission. Gloria was also thirty-eight weeks pregnant and wore a white lab coat that barely covered her bulging belly.

"Julius is coming," Gloria said to Mary, her voice a thin wisp.

The notable glimmer in her eyes would become a doting sparkle when the director arrived later. Mary was sure this infatuation was the reason the clever woman put away her moral compass to become the breeding mare for the Project. Where this project was concerned, many people ignored morality, including the Vatican. In fact, when Gloria announced years ago that she could isolate the genome sequence for each deadly sin, the Vatican became the biggest investor with a controlling interest.

Because outside this building, the world was falling apart.

Mary glanced at the two-way window, and her eyes landed on the collection of pebbles she'd brought in, just like the ones she sometimes left at Flint's desk when he wasn't there. The walk from her apartment in the morning took her through a destitute part of town. The pebbles were sourced from a decrepit building crumbling into an old neighborhood garden where children used to play. This morning, she'd picked up a stone from between a homeless man and what may have been a dead body. No one cared, but she wanted to remind herself of a better future for the children—one where a garden like that had flourished, not degraded.

The world had changed in the past decade. The selfie generation grew up, and with them the sin of greed exploded on a catastrophic scale. Where one sin went, the rest followed. Envy, lust, sloth, wrath, pride, gluttony... even the forgotten deadly sin, despair. Crime became uncontrollable, unrelenting... vicious. Innocent people died every day. Prisons were at capacity. Only last week Mary had seen on the news a teenage boy massacred his family over an argument involving the last piece of pork crackling at the family dinner. Every night there was another story, another death.

The world had gone insane and authorities were at a loss for what to do. That was, until Gloria announced her plan: genetically engineer soldiers capable of sensing deadly levels of sin. They could prevent crime rather than clean up the mess afterwards. That was her dream. It was Julius's dream, too, but after his daughter and wife died from negligent poisoning by a corporation—sloth—he lost his patience. As the years went on, more and more investors joined the Project, each of them having a different idea of how the children would be used. They wanted soldiers. More fighters. Their answer was to meet violence with violence. Sin for sin.

"Yes, Julius is coming," Mary agreed, a bitter taste now in her mouth. "And he's bringing people you won't like."

Mary's vision had shown that Julius was forming a splinter cell of the company, one that believed the world was dying a slow death and putting sinners out of their misery was the only hope of survival. They called themselves the Syndicate. If Mary didn't get the children out now, they would be used in the most horrific way.

Gloria looked at the second scientist. "Mao, I think we're done for the day. You can go home."

"No, wait," Mary said. Gloria frowned at her. This wasn't part of the plan, but... "Before you leave, there is someone I need you to bring here. Flint Fydler from the tech department. He's tall, bearded, wears a baseball cap. Hard to miss."

Mao darted a nervous glance between Gloria and Mary. "It's nine in the morning. Are you sure you want me to go home?"

"Yes," Gloria said, following Mary's lead. "After you deliver Flint to us."

Mary exhaled in relief. They'd talked at length about the plan and possible variables, but sometimes Gloria missed social queues.

Gloria was the surrogate and lead geneticist on the Project. Despite donating her eggs, she refused to be called the mother because she had no contact with the children. Their loud and sudden noises flustered her. In fact, much about the children flustered her, so she watched and recorded from behind the two-way mirror. Gloria was the only person in this godforsaken place who knew and supported Mary's plan to extricate the children.

It hadn't been easy convincing Gloria. It had taken most of the two years, many demonstrations of predictions, and in the end, Gloria respected Mary's gift. She said magic was just science we didn't understand yet. Much of the work Gloria did seemed like magic to Mary, including what she was doing right now.

"Is there anything else, Mao?" Gloria asked.

Mao lifted his eyebrows and returned his clipboard to the bench before exiting the room.

FIVE

FLINT

WHEN FLINT HAD ARRIVED at his desk, he took off his hat and set about his routine. Every day he did the same things. Started his computer, popped in some mint chewing gum, tidied his papers and machine parts, answered his emails, and filled out his schedule in his daily planner. And lastly, he touched each of the smooth pebbles Sister Mary had gifted him and made sure they sat in order of size, from biggest to smallest.

He'd started his collection by picking up flat smooth rocks on his morning run. Mary must have seen his collection, or perhaps he'd mentioned his strange fascination once in the coffee room, because she dropped off pebbles when she thought no one was watching. Except, her pebbles had hidden messages painted underneath them. Usually just a casual quote, or joke... nothing to show it was her, but Flint had caught her on the security tapes. She never mentioned the rocks, so he didn't ask, thinking it was just another secret between them.

Flint liked to leave boxes of chocolates and treats in the fridge labeled innocently as *Sister Mary's, don't touch!* Today it was the chocolate pudding.

Remembering the fallen paper that had escaped Mary's pocket in the lobby, Flint pulled it out and opened it. Gibberish. Code.

He frowned.

Was this another secret between them, or something else?

A loud sound at another desk had him packing the coded letter away. He had no time now. First, there was footage to erase. Then, the final diagnostics on his new disruptor gadget, a round metal sphere. Ten o'clock was only an hour away, and the boss would be in.

The device was perfect. It worked as planned.

He had to show Barry.

Flint navigated back to the lab nearest the reception area. His friend Barry bustled about his station, laying metallic tools and supplies on the bench. Barry was a few years younger than Flint, shorter too. He was part Indian, part British, part douchebag because what he lacked in centimeters, he more than made up for in brains and had the ego to match. No one else in this lab was smarter than him—except maybe Gloria. No one else put up with Flint's grump and snark, but Barry did. That's because his snark was just as good.

They'd been friends since Barry and Flint sat in the same group interview room eight years ago. They had asked the thirty people in the room a series of stupid questions, like—what sound does a dog make, then asked to do the sound. Most people barked like dogs, but not Barry and Flint. Instead, they asked divergent questions like, is the dog from this planet? What breed of dog is it. Is it a real dog, or inanimate? Barry and Flint were the only two to get the job. That was eight years ago.

A familiar pang sliced through Flint's chest and suddenly, he was back there—eight years earlier and just after the worst decision in his life. Just before he got the job at Biolum Industries, he'd been out drinking with a buddy. When it was time to go home, he'd been so intoxicated he could barely stand straight, but he'd still had the sense to think, *We shouldn't drive home.* Pity his sense didn't extend to his mouth. He should have stopped his friend, but his mother's home was only five minutes down the road, and Flint was too lazy to drive another five minutes to his apartment.

The next morning, Flint's shrill phone had woken him up. He still remembered the pause the police woman gave before she spoke, and the sound of a kettle whistling in his mother's kitchen. After dropping Flint off, his buddy had continued on and crashed into a car, killing himself and a mother and father, leaving a baby girl orphaned.

Not a day went by that he didn't regret his negligence. He played scenarios over in his head. What if he'd said for his friend to stay at his for the night? What if he'd called him a cab? He could have taken his keys... she'd still have her parents, maybe a brother or sister... No amount of money could make up for that loss, but when he'd heard about Biolum Industries and their humanitarian project, Flint had signed up the very next day so he could forward most of his paycheck to the orphaned girl. That pang stabbed again. He'd probably always feel it, but each time he sent money to that child, it eased a little more.

"Greetings and salutations," Barry said as he lifted the lid on a glass cylinder filled with a preserved specimen. Ethanol or some other alcoholic fragrance filled the air as it splashed over the rim and onto Barry's white lab coat.

Flint almost gagged. "Shit, how can you stand that smell?"

"How can you stand the smell of melted metal when you're soldering?"

"I use a mask."

"Yeah, well, this isn't toxic, just stinky."

Flint waved his hand across his nose and watched in fascination as his friend pulled a lifeless form out of the cylinder with tweezers and laid it on a metallic pad. Amphibian.

"What is it?" Flint asked as he reorganized Barry's tools without permission. He couldn't help it. Barry was a mess.

"This, my good friend, is a Hairy Frog," Barry declared.

Flint laughed. "Okay, I can see it's hairy, but what's it called?"

"Its scientific name is *Trichobatrachus Robustus*. Highly terrestrial, carnivorous and... see those?" Barry lifted a front limb with the tweezers. "Bone claws that extend from its fingertips when under attack. When they retract, the damaged tissue regenerates. Magic."

"Cool."

"Not as cool as this." Barry pulled another jar from a shelf lined with specimens. He unscrewed the cap and lifted out another slimy slug like creature. "This is an Axolotl. It can regenerate complete body parts—even major organs like a brain. And that slimy slug-face over there is a *Tardigrade* or Water Bear as it's more commonly known." Barry's intelligent eyes held Flint's for dramatic effect. "It can survive for up to one hundred and twenty years without food, invulnerable to freezing or boiling, and can withstand six times the equivalent of the ocean's pressure."

Flint whistled in awe, then placed his gadget on the bench. "But can it disrupt three floors of tech like this?"

"No shit? Three floors?"

"Yup. I'm gonna get the bonus."

"I disagree. I haven't even shown you the best part." Barry bent low to a fridge wedged beneath the lab bench and opened the door. He pulled out a jar with a child-sized human hand floating in the fluid.

"*Jaysuz.*" Flint flinched. "What the hell, bro?"

"Oh, it's not real. Well, it is. But I grew it." Barry placed the jar with the hand specimen on the countertop next to the others. He eyed it like a proud papa bear. "Isn't she beautiful?"

"You grew that?"

"Yep. I combined the stem cells Gloria supplied and grafted a combination of spliced DNA from—"

Flint held up his hand, stopping Barry in his tracks. "Spare me the details. Cut to the chase."

Barry laughed. "It's not new knowledge. Scientists have been able to replicate body parts in jars for years, but... I can grow you another body part at ten times the normal speed. You lose an arm, I'll get you a new one in two years."

"Shit, you will win the bonus. And I really need it." Flint needed a new tire. He needed to put away extra money. College was expensive. He only had a handful of years before he had to think about that. The orphaned girl would need help.

"Shut it," Barry added. "You know how good your shit is. You're only here because my desk is the closest to the Project door."

"You ever wonder what's going on in there?" Flint nodded at the frosted door behind the reception area. It was only a few yards away.

Barry snorted. "Nope. Don't care, mate. I got my own problems to work out. Like how to stabilize the rate of cellular division at a certain marker in time because, at the moment, the limb just keeps growing until adult size, then shrivels and dies." Barry scratched his brown hair, gaze turning inward. "I'm almost there, I can feel it."

Flint's mood picked up. Maybe he'd win the bonus after all. He glanced back at the frosted glass door behind reception. They got paid the best in there, and it was where he aspired to be. He didn't even know if they needed someone like him in there, but he had to try. For college tuition.

"The nuns walk in fresh," Flint said, "and then walk out frazzled. I don't get it. Why would they need nuns? And why do they look so exhausted when they come off shift? And, speaking of that, why do they work in shifts? Around the clock. Morning. Night. Behind guarded doors."

"Well, if you ever get level six clearance, you can tell me. Until then, I have to finish." After a moment, Barry lifted his head. "You going to stand there all day?"

"What? No... I just..."

"You wanted a glimpse of your gorgeous nun."

Heat flared up the back of Flint's neck and his temper returned. "She's hiding something."

"Her double D cups?"

"I'm serious, bro."

"Me too. Go away. I want to make progress before the boss gets here."

"I have theories."

"I know about your theories. I've heard about them for the past eight years."

Flint leaned on the counter and poked the dead frog leg with his pointer. "Come on, Barry. Don't tell me you're not curious about what we're doing here."

"Get your finger off my Hairy Frog."

"Sorry." Flint took his hand back.

Barry took a deep breath. "You're trying to bait me, and it won't work. I don't ask questions because questions get you fired. You remember what happened to Josie down in receiving last year."

Flint bit his lip. "Yeah. Actually, no, she just disappeared. But I guess that's the point."

"Just be happy knowing that we're working toward a better future."

"But, bio-tech-weapons?"

Barry shrugged. "We don't know that."

"What else does a company with a genetics lab, weapons workshop, and armed guards make?"

"Would it make a difference?" Barry asked. "If you knew what was going on behind the door? You still need your money, yeah? Now, enough of your blabbering. Push off before I run out of time to sort out my presentation."

"Fine." Flint picked up his gadget but stopped. Someone was coming out of the Project room.

It was Mao, one Gloria's assistants. Flint didn't get along with Mao. He didn't get along with many people, but especially the scientists who worked with Gloria. They weren't talkative, and when you wanted to probe them for secretive Project information, it made for awkward conversations.

When Mao reached the reception desk, he asked Lizzy something. She pointed in Flint's direction. Mao's eyes met

Flints. Oh no. Did he do something wrong? Did the Sister snitch about the elevator? He shouldn't have made Mary touch him inappropriately. *Dick move.*

Mao broke eye contact first and walked over.

"What do you want?" Flint asked before Mao spoke.

Barry glanced up, noticing the newcomer.

"Gloria would like to speak with you," Mao answered.

"When?" Flint asked.

"Now. In the lab."

Both Flint's and Barry's eyes widened.

"In the lab?" Flint confirmed. "As in, *her* lab?"

"Behind the Project door?" Barry added.

"Yes. Follow me, thank you."

"But it's—"

"Just go, Flint," Barry urged. His unsaid words hung in the air. Flint might not get another chance to see what's behind the door.

SIX

FLINT

FLINT FOLLOWED MAO PAST RECEPTION, beyond the frosted barrier and down a corridor where two GI Joes guarded a door. Man, they were bad-asses. Neither blinked until Mao explained Flint's purpose for being there, and then they sized him up. It seemed Gloria was the magic word. Mao used the retinal scanner and the door behind them opened.

Inside was another lab, much like Flint had imagined. Two desks with a computer sat near a medical bed surrounded by surgical equipment. Shelves with more animal specimens. Insects. Slimy things. Furry things. A small kitchenette to another side. Bright LED lighting throughout. The room was a cross between a research laboratory and an operating theater.

What really surprised Flint was the two-way mirror on the far wall and the empty living quarters behind it.

Then he saw.

Baby bassinets and cots. Four of them, lined in a row, and another three small beds. Seven in total. His gut wrenched and his gaze traveled over the room. What the—?

"Thank you, Mao," came a feminine voice from Flint's side, making him jolt. "You can leave."

Flint's gaze swung to his left where Gloria stood. He was struck by her beautiful skin so pale he could almost see through it. Probably from hours spent working indoors. Maybe a few exfoliations. Whatever women did. Her eyes rivaled the Sister's in size and, yet, it fit together with her wide lips perfectly. Too perfect. It was the kind of beauty that made it hard to form lasting connections. Women wanted to be her, and men wanted to keep her... and then his eyes snagged on her swollen belly and his already twisted gut pulled into a knot. Fuck. Shit. He had a bad feeling about this. The pregnancy. The children's furniture...

But then, Sister Mary Margaret stepped up and smiled at him, and his unease relaxed. Hers was a different kind of beauty to Gloria. She was calming, natural, confident. Surely if a nun was involved in this project, it couldn't be all bad.

Mao left the room, leaving a charged atmosphere.

Flint fumbled with the gadget in his pocket.

"Please, sit," Gloria said and gestured to a chair at her desk. With the help of the Sister, she lowered her awkward body into her seat and then patted the nun's hand. "Thank you, Mary."

Flint noticed straight away that Gloria omitted the nun's official title. Just Mary? What the fuck was going on?

Mary gave Gloria a sweet smile and took a position behind her, standing at her shoulder like a soldier on guard.

Flint sat down as indicated. His grip on his gadget tightened. His knuckles whitened.

"Why am I here?" he asked.

"You are here, Mr. Fydler, because we want to hire you." Gloria opened a notebook on her desk and wrote down something on a blank page. His name. The date. A bullet point.

He frowned. "Aren't I already employed by Biolum Industries?"

"This is true, but... call this a promotion then."

Flint's immediate elation was dampened with logic. Something felt off about this. The gnawing feeling inside didn't like what he saw through that two-way. If he worked here, what would he have to become?

"Despite receiving a glowing recommendation from Mary, I need to do my due diligence. I'd like to ask you a few questions, first. Make sure you are the right man for the job."

Flint's eyebrows lifted and he glanced at Mary. A glowing recommendation? For a brief moment his disbelief was tempered as she held his gaze with steady eyes, but then she glanced at Gloria's notes.

This must be some weird, whacked out dream because there was no way in hell he'd work for a company making children in some evil Dr. Seuss lab. There was no way Mary would be involved in something like that. Doubt danced around the edges of his mind. That coded letter... What if he was wrong?

"Please tell me about yourself, Mr. Fydler—"

"Flint, please."

"—okay, Flint." Gloria wrote, taking special care to dot the i and cross the t.

He shifted in his seat. "What do you want to know?"

"Start with how long you've been working at Biolum?"

"Since the Project started. Eight or so years."

Gloria scribbled. "And what is it you do here?"

Flint frowned. "You want to give me a promotion, but you don't know what I do?"

Aw shit. He needed to get out of here right now.

Gloria cocked her head, watching Flint with curiosity. She stilled for a moment, thinking, and then said, "The truth is, that you're here because of your relationship with Mary."

"What?"

Was it that obvious? Did everyone know how he felt about Mary? Heat prickled his skin. His beard got itchy and he scratched. Shit.

"We need someone we can trust, and Mary trusts you," Gloria added. "But if you could continue answering the question, please?"

"Ah. Okay. I have a double degree in mechanical engineering and computer science. I started with the company as Tech Support and now I'm in Research and Development." He lifted his spherical gadget from his pocket. "I make anything from weapons, to... things like this. It's a disruption device. Set it off and it will shut down anything electrical within a thirty foot radius. That's about three levels high." Flint realized he was about to launch into a tech-nerd explanation of the device and stopped himself. Both Gloria and the sister watched him patiently.

When it was clear he wasn't going to elaborate, Gloria continued. "How much do you know about the Project, Flint?"

"Um. I know as much as anyone else with level five clearance. We were told it's a humanitarian initiative. That we're building tools to help make the world a safer place. That's why I applied. I want to be part of something good." He wanted to do something right after failing so hard when he was younger. He never wanted to feel that guilt wrenching his heart in two. He wanted to be part of the cure, not the disease.

Mary's lips curled up and a light entered her eyes. Call him hopeful, but it looked like pride. A warm feeling spread from his center, washing out his nerves. How did she do it? Every damn time. A smile from her was like a warm hug on a cold day. He wanted more.

Frowning, Gloria gave a soft grunt of discomfort and rubbed her belly. "Apologies, he's kicking. Feisty little one."

"He likes the sound of Flint's voice," Mary said, shifting her smile downward to Gloria's belly.

Gloria's lips quirked on one side. "Or he just wakes up when I'm still."

"No, I think the deep rumble is soothing," Mary added. "Enticing even. Not something he'd normally hear around here."

Flint shifted in his seat. They were discussing timbre of his voice like he wasn't there.

Gloria flicked a glance his way, proving he was wrong. "And what of your future plans?"

"My future?"

"Yes, where do you see yourself in five years? Even two?"

"I... ah... I'm just trying to save enough money to put someone through college." It slipped out before he could stop it.

Gloria looked up sharply, catching his eyes.

Behind her, Mary flinched. "You have a child?" she asked.

"No, but I..." He scrubbed his face. He didn't want to confess his worst sin, but he couldn't lie.

"Mr. Fydler," Gloria said in a clipped voice. "This job will be handsomely rewarded. If it's money you're looking for, we can help with that. But if you have other family commitments, I'm not sure this is for you."

Flint could feel the weight of the Mary's stare on his heated face. He swallowed. "I have no family commitments. This is something else, righting a wrong I made a long time ago." He had no idea why he confessed. He didn't think he wanted the job if it had something to do with weapons and children. But when neither woman spoke, Flint begrudgingly continued. "I could have stopped an accident years ago. Because I didn't, a young girl lost her parents. I send her money every month to help with living expenses."

Gloria put her pencil down, and said, "I don't understand. How could you have stopped it?"

"I knew the driver was getting into his car drunk, and I didn't stop him."

"You didn't tell him to stop?"

"Worse. I thought about it, but said nothing." There. There it was. They knew the worst about him now. Flint studied his gadget, turning the metal sphere in his hands, waiting for the hate.

A soft sigh came from Mary, and he knew there would be pity in her eyes if he looked up. But it was Gloria who spoke in her blunt way. "We all make mistakes. What is important is that we learn from them. I don't believe spending a lifetime sending her money teaches the right lesson, do you?"

Was she belittling his actions? "But I had a responsibility to prevent the tragedy, and I didn't."

Gloria's lips widened, splitting her face in a full smile. Was this woman for real? She twisted and reached up to latch onto Mary's offered hand. Something passed between them until the sound of a crying baby brought everyone's gaze to the window where an older woman walked into the room with a screaming infant.

"Right," Gloria said quickly. "We're running out of time. I think Mary is right. You are the man for the job. Please join me at the observation window." With Mary's assistance, Gloria levered herself out of the chair awkwardly. As they walked to the window, Gloria continued speaking. "What I'm about to tell you mustn't leave this room. Do you understand?"

Flint could only nod. That twisted feeling in his gut hadn't left, and at the sight of the child, it pulled and yanked until he felt physically ill.

"We feel the same way about prevention, Mr. Fydler. When I was a child, I was... hard to control. My parents argued a lot. My father pushed me academically, believing my behavioral problems were because my brain needed stimulation, but my mother disagreed. She believed the smarter I got, the more eccentric I would be, and the less I would fit into society. She wanted a normal life for me. Pride turned their marriage into a battleground until my sixth birthday." She took a deep breath, her sight turning inward. "They argued. So much. It went for hours. *You're the reason no one turned up—You're the problem! She'd have friends if it weren't for you...*" The tone of Gloria's voice became tighter, strained as she mimicked her parents' argument, and then all emotion leached from her voice. "My father shot my mother in front of me, and then he shot himself. Point blank." Gloria stopped. She put her hand to the window and stared, watching the nun inside placate the baby until its cries softened, and it eventually fell asleep on her shoulder.

Well fuck, thought Flint. That was a shitty childhood. But what did it have to do with anything?

The silence expanded. Flint turned to look at Mary and found she already watched him.

"Ten years ago," Gloria continued, "I isolated the genome sequence for greed. Once I'd done that, the rest of the deadly sins weren't hard to find. And then I met Julius. He was devastated after his wife and child were poisoned and together we thought, wouldn't it be magical if we could stop these sins before they happened? Of course, you know what magic is, don't you Flint?" Gloria gave him a wry smile. "It's science we don't understand yet."

The room in front of them suddenly filled with children ranging from elementary grade to toddler. All looked similar in features, wide lips, big eyes, darkish hair... features he had no doubt would develop into the painted perfection of their mother. He detected a few lighter splashes of hair color and tanned skin. Who was the father? It didn't matter. Flint didn't need to know. He didn't need any of this.

"Each of these precious children has had their DNA tweaked and modified so they can sense deadly levels of sin. They are the first of their kind. Maybe the last."

"You're making super soldiers," Flint stated. He could

feel the heat rising up his neck, the anger prickling his skin. "You're experimenting on innocent children, forcing them into a life none of them asked for."

"They're well looked after," Gloria started, but then held her tongue. Irritation swam on her features and she avoided his eyes. She stepped away from the mirror, rubbing her belly, breathing deep. Something Flint said clearly distressed her.

"That's why we're here." Mary stepped in. "The Vatican is a major investor and insisted they were the humanitarian representation. We nuns are responsible for the wellbeing of the children. You can see they're treated well. They're not harmed in any way. All tests are done by saliva swab, nothing intravenous."

An older boy smacked a younger boy on the head and snatched his stick of celery back. A fight almost broke out, but the eldest girl, maybe six or seven, stepped in and soothed them all. She was tall and waif-like, like her mother.

"That's Despair," said Gloria, back at Flint's side. "Despite her namesake, she's always stepping in to keep the peace. It's the forgotten deadly sin, yet, I believe the most important. Hope is her virtue. She astounds me every time. And those two she interrupted"—she pointed—"Wrath and Gluttony."

Christ. They didn't even have real names, like mass-produced products on an assembly line. "They're not machines, you know. What if they grow up and decide not to be your peace-keepers? What if they want something else for their lives? What if hunting sin wears down on them, twists them, and turns them into the very thing they're fighting against?"

Both women stared at him.

"That's exactly why you're here," Gloria said simply.

Flint opened his mouth to respond but shut it in confusion. This was all getting too much. Too many variables. Not like a computer system where everything was zeros and ones. Where it had to be either one or the other. This had the potential for chaos.

"Julius has changed," Gloria whispered. Her words cut through Flint's confusion with a slice of danger.

"The boss? What do you mean?"

"At the start of this, he wanted to prevent loss of life, but now... now he wants to control the children and use them for his own gain. The bitterness of losing his first wife and child has twisted him into something ugly. I thought making him the sperm donor for these children would give him purpose again, but it's all messed up now. I was so wrong. He pushed me to make them better, stronger, more powerful than anyone could hope. He thinks he owns them." She took a deep breath and sighed. "I told him I could give them enhanced abilities to help with their jobs, to give them an advantage over the criminals... but none of the abilities have manifested, and the investors are getting restless. The children's lives are in danger. If I can't demonstrate their investment is advancing, they'll be wiped out."

"We won't let that happen," Mary said, placing a firm hand on Gloria's shoulder.

"How the hell are you going to stop them?" Flint shook his head in disbelief. "You're a bunch of nuns and a skinny-ass pregnant woman. I can't help. I'm not a fighter.... I..."

"I'll pay you a million dollars for each child," Gloria blurted out. "To help get them safely to the Hildegard Abbey, where Mary is from."

"Fuck." Flint's gaze shot to Mary. He liked her, he really did, but how could he be part of this? "Fuck. I can't. I'm just a guy."

He couldn't even save one child, let alone many.

The room swayed. He had to get out of there.

SEVEN

MARY

MARY SENSED Flint's panic rise and rushed to his side, placing hands on his shoulders. In his eyes, she searched for understanding, but found only fear.

"Flint..." She took a deep breath, unsure how to proceed without scaring him off. She was about to tell him everything and prayed to the Virgin Mary that he could take it. Mary glanced at Gloria. "Could you please give us a few minutes, Gloria?"

Gloria placed her hand on her stomach and nodded. "I will go to the bathroom. When I get back, Flint, I need an answer. We are almost out of time."

Something hardened in Gloria's eyes before she left. Her insinuation was clear. Mary would have to deal with Flint if he said no, and she didn't want to do that.

He *had* to say yes. He wouldn't have been in her recent vision if he said no... would he?

"You're more than just a guy, Flint," Mary said, sliding her hands down his arms, tracking the movement with her eyes. *Sweet Mother.* She knew she shouldn't be touching him, but she loved those arms. Her fingers ran back up to his shoulders. "Flint, you're much more than that to me. You're loyal, determined, clever... exactly the person we need to help get us out of this. I've *seen* it."

He gave her a pained look. "Sister..."

"I'm not a nun," she blurted, dropping her hands from him.

He blinked, spluttered. "What?"

"I..." Mary surveyed the room on instinct, making sure no one watched. It was an old habit when you lied about your identity. One that stayed even though she knew they were alone. "I'm not a nun. The others in there are, but I'm... a Sinner. I'm part of a secret faction in the Hildegard Sisterhood that even the Vatican doesn't know about."

"Tell me about them."

"The Sisterhood?"

"The secret faction."

She took a deep breath. "They have a history reaching back to medieval times when the original Sister Hildegard struggled against a male dominated clergy. Now the world knows Hildegard as the founder of scientific history in Germany, but back then, her opinions were completely disregarded until she claimed to have visions from God himself. Belittling herself as a woman in order to be heard was only the beginning of the humiliation the woman faced.

"So she started her own abbey filled with women. That same abbey exists today and is a place where women can be celebrated and their education encouraged—minus the male influence. Records at the Sisterhood archives reveal they had a hand in the rise to power of many women over history from Joan of Arc to Indira Gandhi. From Catherine the Great to Margaret Thatcher. But, under the surface of the auspicious abbey is their secret mission that no woman should ever suffer the same struggle as Hildegard had."

"So you hate men?"

"No! Maybe some of them do, but I can't. Not with someone like you in my life."

Flint ran his hands through his hair. "There's more you're not telling me. What is this sinner business? How does their mission to put women in power relate to this project?"

"They want women to influence the children, and... well, there are things holy women can't do, and that's what I'm for. I'm allowed to sin. In fact, I'm the designated sinner —their necessary evil. My line of work isn't exactly inno- cent, so I'm not ordained and my vows are different to allow me the freedom to work. I guess I'm more like a CIA opera- tive, if you like. I'm sorry I lied to you. It's cut me up inside for months, but I couldn't jeopardize my purpose for being here. The fewer who know, the better."

She turned her gaze to the two-way mirror and held her

breath, waiting for a reaction from Flint. Something. Anything.

Silence.

And then he moved, cutting into her personal space.

No man in the world intimidated Mary. None. Yet, she found herself back against the wall with Flint dominating the area before her. His body heat hit her in the face, stealing her air, making it hard to breathe. She closed her eyes to steady her beating heart. One. Two. She opened them.

"Are you fucking shitting me?" he bit out. The crease between his brows deepened, the two slashes of brown almost one. His lashes lowered as he took in her face, coming to terms with her confession. "So I was right. You're not a goddamned nun."

She licked her lips and, on instinct, lifted her finger to smooth the wrinkle still between his brow. She hated knowing she put that there. There was a small smudge of grease on the bridge of his nose, and Mary rubbed it away. His eyes fluttered closed, and he leaned in to her touch. When they opened, some revelation flashed in his eyes. It was deep, dark, carnal and desperate. He cupped her face between his hands and lowered his lips to press against hers reverently.

His salty taste hit Mary's senses and desire sparked an inferno inside. Everything she'd held back over the years came rushing to the surface. She speared her fingers into his hair, pulled him close, and returned the flames. Everything she'd denied, she pushed into that kiss. She had to let him know how she felt, how she truly felt. No more teasing. No more flirting. She needed him with every ounce of her being. She pushed her tongue into his, bit his lip, sucked, licked, kissed. He got it all.

Breathing hard, Flint pushed his hard body against hers, flattening her against the wall, trapping her. *Sweet Mother,* this was what she wanted. Needed. This was exactly what she'd imagined. His taste, heat, passion... all funneled in her direction, as though she were the only thing in his life worth having. His tongue delved inside her mouth, claiming and taking. She released a small moan of appreciation. He swallowed it with another kiss. Yes. More. Together.

He pulled back suddenly and the cold air rushed in. His hair stood up, mussed from her fingers, looking every bit disheveled as she felt. All that heat, all that fire, gone in an instant and she was left bereft and trembling.

"Flint?" she asked, voice as shaky as her legs.

"I've wanted to do that since I met you." It was an accusation. He scrubbed his face and turned his back on her. He clenched his fists at his side. She placed a palm between his shoulder blades and he shuddered. "How can I trust you," he murmured, "when you've lied to me the entire time I've known you?"

Her head dropped next to her hand and she sighed, resting her cheek on his warm back. There was nothing more she wanted to do than slide her hands around his waist and hug him tight. "I'll tell you anything you want to know. Anything."

He turned and held her at arm's length. "Start with the elevator. Why did you want me to delete the camera footage—which I did, by the way, and you're welcome. You can thank me later."

"Part of what I told you wasn't a lie. They don't like weakness around here. If they found out I had a condition, they'd fire me. But the truth is, there's more to it. It's not epilepsy. I have visions," she said, squeezing her eyes shut. *Here goes.* "Please believe me. I'm not lying. As far-fetched as it sounds, I can see the future. If Julius found out, my mission would be in jeopardy."

"Your mission?"

"The children." Mary nodded at the observation window where the children were now helping to clean up their meals.

"Jesus fucking Christ, Mary. Am I part of your mission?"

"No! God no. I never meant to involve you, but... *¡Ay, chingado!* I make the worst nun because I can't stay away from you. My feelings were bound to come out. From the first time we bumped into each other in the break room to the time you started leaving me sweets. I've loved our talks. Nobody has ever cared enough to ask me about my day, but you do. I think about you all the time, and I've dreamed about what it would be like if I were a normal woman. But,

I'm not. You endanger my mission, just by being a variable I haven't planned for. But I ... it's you."

She gestured up and down his magnificent body. He wasn't a body builder by any means, but he was trim, fit, sexy as hell, and all she could think about. Living with nuns for two decades had seriously depleted her opportunities for male company.

"Yeah. It's me." Pure male ego infused his words. He pulled her back into his arms, a slow smile creeping up his face. "I knew you couldn't resist my charms."

She slapped him playfully on the chest. "You're such an ass."

"You love it. You keep coming back for more."

Mary sighed. That was the Flint she missed. She traced his short beard with her finger, feeling along the line of his strong jaw. His eyes sparkled under his long lashes and she knew in that moment she wanted him with her, always, in all futures. She shivered at the thought of her visions. "Maybe I do, but I wasn't wrong when I said I had a mission. I've seen two futures. One where they're used for evil, the other where they're used for good."

Flint went quiet. Still. Tension creeped into his posture and Mary felt it through his arms. "Flint?"

"Mary. I don't know if I can help you. I don't agree with them being used at all."

"It's a little late for that. They're here. They've been created. I wasn't a part of that but if they're not guided in the right direction, then we're all doomed. Flint," Mary pleaded. "This is your chance to prevent more pain. You ignored your instincts once, don't do it again. Help me save them."

Her words cut him. Pain flickered in his eyes one minute, gone the next. "But why me? What do I have to offer? I'm useless in relationships, to people. I fuck up and people get hurt. Jesus, part of the reason I chased you was because I knew I could never have you. And now... I don't know." He stepped away from her.

She studied her feet. "Since I saw your face in the vision, I've asked myself the same thing. I thought, why Flint? Maybe it's your tech skills, or maybe my feelings tainted the vision. I had a plan that would work fine. I thought I was all they needed, then... in the lift... you smiled at me that way, you boxed me in against the wall and I let you. We touched, and—" Their eyes met. "Something changed between us. Something shifted. Don't tell me you didn't feel it."

"Oh, I felt it all right. And I felt like a complete moron getting a hard-on over a nun." He rubbed his chin. "I'll tell you what. It sure feels good knowing I'm not going to hell anymore."

"Does this mean you'll help?"

He refocused on Mary. "Tell me about the letter."

"Letter?" As the word came out of her mouth, a cold pit dropped in her stomach.

"The one that dropped from your pocket in the security line this morning. Someone wrote it in code."

"How do you know it's mine?"

An eyebrow arched. "Are you still lying?"

Mary pinched the bridge between her nose. "Yes."

"Last chance, Mary. I want all your cards on the table. If we want trust between us, it has to be that way. I can't handle lies. What was the letter about?"

He was right. If she wanted something real between them, she had to go all in. Mary steeled herself. This went against protocol, but she found she couldn't lie to him anymore. She didn't want to. Even if he ended up hating her for it. What they had was the only real thing in her life, and the lies had tainted it.

"I have told no one this. Not even Gloria." Her hand hovered over the queasiness in her belly. Here goes. "It was instructions from my superior regarding the mission. If I can't get the children to the safety of the Sisterhood Abbey, then... she wants me to destroy everything. Including them."

His eyes flashed wide. "You can't be serious. Mary. You're not entertaining the idea, are you?"

She bit her lip. "This is what I've trained for, Flint. I'm their sinner. I don't like it. But... I don't know what else to do."

"Mary." His voice softened like a caress. "No. You're *not* that person, do you hear me? I know you. You're not evil. You're the woman who brings me cute little rocks and secretly puts them on my desk. I can see the same collection of pebbles and rocks in there with the children. You care for those kids, I know you do. You have hope for a future where killing isn't the answer."

Tears burned her eyes. "You knew the pebbles were from me?"

"I can hack into the camera feed, remember?"

She blushed, blinking away wetness.

"My point is," he continued. "You're thoughtful. You're caring. You're not a killer of innocents. I don't care what they call you, *you're not evil*. Please believe that."

"So help me get them out of here. Help us destroy the research so it can't be repeated."

Flint didn't have time to respond. A commotion at the security door brought both their attentions there.

Gloria strode in—actually, it was more like a fierce waddle. Her stomach was so big compared to her thin body, it threw her balance off. Her white lab coat was buttoned over her breasts but flared over her bulge, accentuating the pregnancy.

Mary's stomach dropped when she saw the man walking in behind Gloria. Julius. A tall, handsome, sophisticated nightmare on legs. Mary saw his face frequently in her visions, always accompanied by blood and tears. She couldn't look him in the eyes without betraying her emotion. To anyone else, he was a successful businessman, a widow and grieving father, but to Mary, he was the precipice the world balanced on. One push and it was the end.

EIGHT

FLINT

FLINT SENSED the boss-man was in a mood the minute he waltzed into the lab. Cut from steel, Julius's face was stern, harsh and prepared for battle. Except, what was he fighting for?

Two men followed Julius into the room. One was brown-skinned and wore an official military uniform. A decorated officer. Older, graying on top, sharp lines around his shrewd eyes. The second man was a Japanese businessman, shorter, but no less imposing. He wore a suit that shouted money, and an aura that screamed importance.

Julius barely glanced at Flint and Mary, but followed Gloria to the viewing window. The other two men joined him. They must assume Flint had clearance to be in there.

When Mary touched his arm in a way that suggested they don't move, he realized he'd been holding his breath.

"As you can see, they're in perfect health," Julius said, waving his arm at the window.

"Yes," said the Japanese man, heavily accented. "But we're not interested in perfect health."

"We want results," the military man concluded.

"Results take time," Gloria said. "We've discussed this."

"And I think we have had enough time," Julius said, his voice eerily calm, as though he knew things no one else did. "We've had eight years of time and all you've got to show are some screaming shit factories who rarely get sick and heal fast. But all we've seen are minor scratches and grazes. You promised more, Gloria. It's time to deliver on that promise."

"We've demonstrated their ability to sense their particular sin with a hundred percent accuracy. You've seen them heal. They're stronger than the average child. They're brighter, smarter... what more do you want?"

"In your investment proposal, you promised they would develop special abilities from the moment they were born," the military man said, dark eyes darting as he recalled. "You sited borrowing skills such as shapeshifting from other creatures. Potential invulnerability. Possible psychic powers, poison production, camouflage and there was another animal sampled... what was it again?"

"Electric Eel," Julius offered.

"Yes. That's right. Electrical powers. As far as I can see, none of that is there."

"I know what I promised." Gloria's shoulders pulled up

tight and her head shook from side to side in a nervous tick. "I'm well aware what was in the proposal."

"So, what evidence can you demonstrate?"

"It's not something we can turn on like a tap." Gloria's head kept shaking, trembling from side to side. "It's not on demand. They're not machines."

"Gloria, focus," Julius said, pursing his lips.

She made a strained sound and squeezed her eyes shut. She took deep breaths and calmed herself. When she met Julius's eyes, her own were unreadable. "The powers will grow with the children. You don't arm a child with a gun, so we don't arm them with deadly powers until they're old enough to handle them. There are protocols. Rules."

"Cut off one of their limbs," declared the Japanese man. "If what you say is true, it will grow back. I want to see this fabled regeneration."

The air solidified in Flint's lungs, and Mary gasped beside him. Gloria's face turned a sickly yellow and for the first time since the men had arrived, she looked to Mary for guidance.

Mary's eyes darkened in a way that Flint had never seen before. Danger thundered in the atmosphere. Her posture stiffened. For the first time, Flint truly believed she wasn't a nun, and something else entirely. What did she call herself? Like a CIA agent?

Who was this woman he had fallen in love with?

Uncertainty swam in his gut, but she'd told him the truth when he'd asked. That wouldn't have been easy. For all she knew, he could have exposed her truth the before Flint wearing a suit and tie.

Mary gave Gloria an almost imperceptible nod.

The fear faded from Gloria's eyes and she jutted out her chin. "I'm not torturing these children."

"They're not children. They're experiments. And we own them," Julius clipped. "You'll do as you're told, otherwise we'll end this all right now. They have wasted enough resources. We can start again, assess your research, work out what went wrong and... Gloria. Are you listening?"

But Gloria was bending over, clutching her stomach, groaning. Her face had screwed up, and she developed a labored breathing pattern.

"Contraction," she bit out.

Mary launched from Flint's side and went to Gloria, smoothly nabbing something from a lab countertop. Nobody else saw, but Flint did. She hid it behind her back in a stealthy move.

"She's going into labor," Mary said and shouldered her way to Gloria's side. "Give her space."

Mary placed her hand at the small of Gloria's back and whispered to her.

Julius's companions grumbled amongst themselves. They glowered in Gloria's direction, but took a step backward. The Japanese man's lips whitened around the edges, as though he were suppressing a tidal wave. Then he couldn't hold it in any longer.

"No," he said. "We will not be deterred. Contractions

can last hours, days even. Once this one is finished, we will continue with the amputation."

"I agree," the military man said. "We've waited too long. I'm flying out of this God-forsaken city tomorrow afternoon and I have to take news back to the Syndicate. They'll want evidence of progress."

"Who is the Syndicate?" Gloria panted.

The military man's face deadpanned. "I don't know what you mean."

"Yes, you do. You said Syndicate. That name doesn't appear in our contract."

Julius nudged the military man out of the way with a disparaging look. "It's just another name for investors, you know that. Now, please can we focus on an amputation."

From the look on Mary's face, it was clear she didn't believe him. Gloria made a pained sound, doubling over, rubbing her underbelly.

Flint had stood still until now, too shocked to move. But these men, they were complete and utter fuckwits. His mouth couldn't form words. Fury licked up his spine, coating his body in trembling waves of heat. The gadget in his pocket felt like the perfect bludgeoning weapon. He could take one of them out, easy. The other two would be harder, but if Mary truly was who she said she was, then between the two of them, they'd be fine.

God, was he even considering this?

Then Flint heard the distinct sound of water splashing, and Gloria's whimpers became a wail.

"Her waters broke," Mary said. "Everyone out!"

Julius's face contorted in rage, and his gaze snapped between his partners. Whatever he'd promised them, he'd have to wait for another day.

"Fine," Julius said to Gloria. "Tomorrow morning we will return." Then he stalked toward the exit, not once taking the time to check on the woman about to give birth.

When all three men vacated, Flint rushed to Gloria's side.

"What can I do?" he asked.

But Gloria stopped panting, stood up straight and gave a big sigh. She patted her head and went to her desk to search through some papers. She calmly picked up the phone receiver and dialed a number. Confused, Flint turned to Mary for answers.

She held up an empty test tube bottle in her hand. "Fake."

"Yes, hello, Dr. Stilenski, it's Gloria. I've gone into labor, can you please come as soon as possible to deliver the baby? Great." She hung up the phone and waddled to the medical bed where she pulled out a drip bag and intravenous kit from a cupboard. "I think it's best we start the oxytocin now. It could be hours before it works."

Mary went to her side and put her hand on the drip bag to stop her. "No. It's too risky. We should continue our plan and leave tonight. You can have the baby at the abbey. It will be safe there."

"Um, excuse me, but what the hell is going on?" Flint asked.

Mary glanced at him. "Flint, we lied about her being in labor."

"I can see that. So what are you doing?"

"Mary," Gloria continued, ignoring Flint, "don't you see? He won't stop coming. He might even be back this afternoon and if there's no baby..."

Shit. Flint scrubbed his face. He felt like he was stuck in some alternate reality. How could he have worked for a company that tortured children?

Mary pushed the IV bag down again. "I'll deal with him then, but running away with a newborn and a woman recovering from childbirth is not good. You could get injured. There are too many variables unaccounted for. What if the birth doesn't go as planned?"

"This is my eighth child. I will be fine."

Gloria slipped the bag from beneath Mary's hands and set about unpacking it.

"Gloria, I can't condone this. I only saw seven children in the vision. You give birth and there will be eight, making everything I've seen about a safe escape null and void. Please don't do it."

Gloria hesitated and contemplated the needle in her hand. It was clear she was distressed, her head trembled from side to side, much like it had when Julius tried to force her to amputate a child's limb. Her brows drew together and she took a shuddering breath.

"It was never supposed to be this way." Tears welled in Gloria's eyes. "It wasn't supposed to be like this."

A bang on the observation window drew everyone's attention. The eldest female child had her palms and forehead plastered to the glass, looking at things she couldn't possibly see through the mirror. She had long, dark hair like her mother. Flint inched his way closer. He sidestepped a lab station, and the girl's eyes tracked him. There was no way she could see him, so how was she doing it? Flint made it to the window, and then the girl's eyes snapped Gloria's way.

"Despair," Mary said, now next to Flint. "Even now she can feel our pain."

A hiss made them turn to find Gloria inserting the intravenous needle into her vein. One handed, she taped it in place and the hung the bag on the hook above the medical gurney before collapsing on it herself.

"No!" Mary ran toward her, but it was too late, the oxytocin flowed into Gloria's veins, inducing the labor. Gloria's hand whipped to her stomach and she grimaced, feeling the pull of her first contraction. "Thy drugs are quick," she whispered, already lost in another world.

Mary placed her hands on the medical bed and bowed her head silently, gathering herself. Despair hit the window again, clanging it repetitively. Flint turned to see a tear sliding down the girl's face, and his throat closed up. This was all wrong.

"Flint." Mary's voice cut through his haze. All traces of her anguish replaced with cold hard determination.

"Yes?"

"We need to know if you're in, or out."

He glanced at the observation window. The girl still watched through the mirrored window, and behind, her siblings played unperturbed by what she sensed. A boy stood on the table, and another was on the floor preparing to catch him. There were discarded pillows and blankets all around to act as cushions. The toddlers crawled, putting the pebbles Mary had brought in their mouths. And the nun on duty checked her watch, waiting for Mary to start her shift. A sharp pain pierced Flint's heart. They were just kids. Goddamned kids who didn't ask for this.

"I'm in," he said. "Whatever you need."

NINE

MARY

MARY CHECKED her watch for the fifth time that night as she waited in the observation room for a signal from Flint, and then it was all systems go. Until then, she waited.

It had been several hours since Gloria gave birth to Envy, a healthy little boy. Now both mother and child rested peacefully. Gloria on the medical gurney, and the baby in a bassinet buggy next to her.

As soon as Dr. Stilinski had turned up, Mary left to take over the day shift in the children's room. Keeping up appearances was essential, especially now. Nobody could suspect their escape, or their plan would be in jeopardy.

After spending hours with the high energy children, Mary was now perfectly primed and ready for the mission. Most people would be drained, but she had trained for this. Instead of exhaustion, she was pumped.

The Sisterhood had filled Mary's life with rigorous

physical exercise and preparation, often under extreme conditions. She'd also been shipped off around the world with other Sinners to learn the Art of Warfare from different cultures, spending up to a year studying under each. She still remembered her harsh endurance training with the Shaolin monks, conditioning parts of her body to be kill-proof. To strengthen her neck to resist chokeholds, she'd hanged from a noose in a tree while completing her postures. She did this for hours a day, weeks at a time. In comparison, looking after screaming children was a cakewalk.

Mary fiddled with the sleeves of her Sinner battle uniform. It had been packed in an emergency backpack hidden under Gloria's desk. Simple nun clothes had been replaced with black pants, jacket, hood and red scarf that stretched to cover her nose and mouth if she needed to hide her identity.

She checked her weapons. Throwing daggers up each sleeve. A fixed blade sheathed in her boot. No guns. They were unpredictable, messy, and not suitable for use around children. After the arsenal check, she took stock of the backpack. There were passports, cash, protein bars and a range of emergency items inside. Flint had been sent to collect the getaway van and other supplies like baby formula and diapers. Mary had always planned on getting the van herself until today. The vision had changed, and Julius has upped the ante.

But they could work this. She trusted her visions. They would survive if they stuck together.

She cracked her neck and checked on Gloria. Still sleeping. Good. She needed to rest for what came next and the hospital gown would suffice for the short trip down to the basement garage.

Mary checked through the observation window and noticed Sister Josephine sitting on a chair, knitting in the dimly lit room. Mary would've preferred one of the younger nuns on for tonight; she would need their strength getting the kids downstairs, but had to roll with what they had.

All children were asleep. Most of the building had gone home. In a few minutes, Flint would arrive downstairs in the garage, and they would put their plan into action.

Nothing to do but wait.

Mary glanced at her cell-phone and checked the time.

Soon.

Her belly flip-flopped at the thought of Flint and she felt like a ridiculous teenager. Since he'd left, half her thoughts had been of him. All that verbal pushing and pulling they'd done for the past two years had finally culminated into something real, and it was more than Mary had hoped for. He felt the same way about her. Enough to risk everything and rescue the children.

That kiss.

The butterflies in her stomach churned. Her fingers fluttered to her lips at the memory, itching to feel his touch again. That pressure, that heated passion. The tickle of his beard against her face. For a moment, Mary allowed herself to imagine what that beard would feel like elsewhere on her body. Rough, light, scratchy? On her bare breasts, her stomach, between her legs. *Sweet Mother*.

In her wildest dreams she'd never factored a relationship into her future. It had always been about the mission. The children. Gloria. Save them, save the world. Flint had faith in her, and she realized she had faith too. The order to eliminate the children had never fully embedded in her brain. With Flint part of her plan now, she'd never need that horrific failsafe. Thank God, her visions were rarely wrong because she couldn't wait for all this to be over, and to get him alone.

"You're thinking of him," Gloria croaked from her bed.

"You're awake." Mary pushed off the bench she'd been resting against and went to Gloria's side. "How are you feeling?"

Mary touched the back of her hand to Gloria's forehead. It was sweaty and clammy and Gloria's hair stuck to her face around the edges. Her eyes had dark circles under them. All of these things made Mary think the birth had been harder than usual. She wished she could have been there for her, but she'd been with the children.

Gloria took Mary's hand from her forehead.

"Do you want water?" Mary asked.

Gloria shook her head. "Tell me about Flint."

"Do you not trust him?"

"No. That's not what I meant. You think about him. I saw your face. You like him. A lot."

A blush heated Mary's cheeks. "I do. I know it's not something we planned for, but I've had feelings for him for a while. It feels good to imagine a future with him in my life." In her bed... "He will help us. I know it. He'll pull through."

"Bring me the laptop."

Mary glanced at the machine on Gloria's desk. "Now?"

"Yes. I want to pay him."

"You can do that later."

"Please," Gloria said in a strained voice. "It has to be now. I don't want a doubt in his mind as to his purpose."

Mary could see Gloria's nervous head-shake developing and didn't want to distress her, so rushed to retrieve the laptop and set it up on Gloria's lap. Within minutes, Gloria transferred money into Flint's payroll account.

"Done. Eight million dollars. You're next."

Mary shook her head. "I don't need your money, Gloria. I'm not doing this for the wealth. The Sisterhood will take care of everything."

"That's why I'm giving it to you, because you don't want it."

"You mean to Flint. You gave it to Flint. I won't give you my bank details."

"Then I'll give the rest to Flint and he can give it to you if you change your mind." A few more clicks on the keyboard. "Done."

There was a flash of emotion in Gloria's eyes as she closed the lid on the laptop. Something coy and knowing. As though she knew the answer to a riddle Mary hadn't asked yet. Then it was gone, quickly replaced by another Mary tried to decipher.

Gloria idly slid her hands back and forth on the smooth laptop surface, thinking, and then dropped her heavy head back to the pillow. When she finally lifted her tired gaze, Mary recognized the turmoil.

A memory clicked.

She'd seen the same tortured look in a comrade during a training exercises in Japan. Mary had tutored under the *Onna Bugeisha*—a powerful secret society of female Samurai. Like the Sisterhood, they were all women. It was what the Sisterhood prided themselves in; secret women's business. Men were a hindrance. Their tempers, their testosterone. *Let them think they rule the world, but behind the scenes, we do.* Women were the brains and the brawn. Slipping in unnoticed for centuries, assassinating and neutralizing threats, then slipping out with their enemy none the wiser. Who would suspect a nun of treachery—of sin?

This one particular time, Mary had been only sixteen or so, and the group of Japanese women she fought with staged a mock battle in the countryside. The first team to get to the other side, and capture the flag, won. Mary's team was down to the last two people—her and a woman named Akari. Their battle had been desperate and two days long. Both girls were at the end of their limits and outnumbered, six to two, but Akari had this look in her eyes. Dark, hollow, determined. If she went down, then she would do it with honor. It was only a mock battle, but the sacrifice was real. She drew the enemy away from Mary which allowed Mary to cross the field and take the flag before anyone noticed. Gloria had the same look in her eyes now.

"Gloria," Mary said, a warning tone in her voice. "What are you thinking?"

"You said your vision changed this morning."

"Yes, Flint was added."

"And who was taken away?"

Mary went cold. "What do you mean?"

"The laws of science say that with every action, there is an equal and opposite reaction. Who was left out?"

Mary frowned. "I-I... I don't know, I haven't... my visions aren't science, more like magic." She was a *Bruja*, that's what the mean children in her youth had teased, it was what her parents had called her. It was the source of all her pain.

"Mary." Gloria's expression was condescending. "I don't have to remind you what I think about magic, now do I? Look now. Think back. Please. It's important."

Mary closed her eyes, centered her breathing, relaxed. To conjure the vision she had in the elevator, she remembered the smells in there. The metallic taint of the steel doors, the musty carpet, freshly showered male... a hint of mint... then the vision came back, flashing and flickering like an old movie reel. One, two... she counted the adult faces she saw, the children, and then—an ache so sharp hit her squarely in the chest. No. It can't be. Shame flamed Mary's cheeks. She'd been so caught up with, so excited about... that she completely focused on the wrong thing. She shook her head. Unbelievable. How could she be so stupid? So negligent? So blind?

The mission came first and she failed.

Gloria was not in the vision.

When Mary reopened her eyes, recognition echoed back at her. She knew. Gloria somehow understood.

"No," Mary said, determined to find a way. "It doesn't matter. That vision is null and void because you had the child. You broke the cycle. Damn it, I should have written it down. Normally I record the vision. I'm so stupid. *Pinche pendejo!*"

"No. You're not." But Gloria's lashes fluttered closed. "You are exactly what the children need. You and Flint. Me, on the other hand... I've never been able to accept the reality of being a mother. They've only been moving pictures behind a window. I'm not capable of more. I know it. Accept it. I've lost too much blood and am too weak to move far. I will slow you down. You must leave me."

Mary's veins turned to stone. "No. I'll wheel you down in the gurney."

"Mary, be realistic. You have eight children to move."

"It doesn't matter, I—"

"You may have to fight."

"I can't—"

"Mary!" Gloria grasped Mary's hand in her own. "There are things I have to tell you. To prepare you for. Listen."

Mary squeezed the tears from her eyes, inhaled deeply and pushed the panic away. She was better than this. She'd trained for worse situations. She was unbreakable.

So don't break.

"Okay. Tell me."

"I lied to Julius."

"About what?"

"The children. Their powers." Gloria licked her lips. Her eyes fluttered. The automatic medicating machine must have released a dose of morphine. She slurred her next words. "They all have them."

"Why aren't they manifesting?"

"Because I blocked them under a layer of their sin's opposing virtue."

"What does that mean?"

"When they meet a mate who embodies their exact opposite, their special ability will manifest, and they'll be able to procreate. It will be safe for them to start their own family," Gloria murmured, then drifted asleep. "I want them to have a full life."

"Gloria, I don't understand." Mary patted Gloria's hand, but she'd gone silent.

Mary's phone pinged, signaling Flint was down in the garage with the van, ready to go. In a few minutes, he'd be finished laying his disrupter devices to wipe the camera feeds. Mary shot a text back to give her five minutes.

"Gloria?" Mary patted her again.

Gloria's eyes opened. "Hmm?"

"You were telling me about the children. What did you mean exactly?"

For the first time in Mary's life, she saw tears in Gloria's eyes.

"Those children will grow to be saviors, but in the wrong hands, they will bring destruction. So, I blocked them from having the ability to have children, and I locked their powers away. Just in case."

In case we fail.

Gloria panted, stressed. "It was always about balance, Mary. There had to be a balance. It's a safety mechanism. I may be a scientist, but I'm not mad. I won't condone bringing evil into the world. My parents had no balance. None. Too wrong for each other, but these children... they have a chance. Never in my life did my parents look at each other the way you and Flint do. With both of you they have a chance." Gloria's grip tightened on Mary's hand. Wild, dark hair fell around her face. She locked eyes with Mary. "Promise me you stick with Flint and show these children what true love looks like, so when they find their mate, they latch on with two hands. They save themselves. Promise me. *Promise* me."

A lump formed in Mary's throat as Gloria's words sank in. Her plea changed everything. No more Sisterhood. No more Plan B where she saved the world by ending the deadly children before they grew up. A life with the children and Flint settled in her mind with a sense of rightness, of possibility. She could teach them everything she knew about warfare, and Flint could teach them how to have a soul. Together, with the right training, the children could grow into the leaders the world needed.

Maybe they could grow a garden. Together.

Mary nodded. "I promise."

Gloria sank in relief. "I've done all I can to help them," Gloria mumbled, darkness swimming over her features yet again. "I made them strong in body, I programmed biological warnings, triggers, pheromones... the Bee Wolf Wasp... but you have to make them strong in heart. I can't. I can't."

Gloria faded for a moment. Mary let go of her hand and paced the room. She made no sense. What the hell? A Bee Wolf Wasp? Mary knew the building was full of research laboratories for this project. Billions of dollars went into it. Billions. There were animals and insects from all over the world, from the highest mountain to the deepest ocean. Cutting edge genome sequencing and engineering. It all went to make these children what they were, except it came to the project room in pieces for Gloria to put together. It was a security strategy—to keep the important information isolated so no one could steal it and understand the master plan.

Mary tried to recalibrate, to adjust the escape. Before Gloria dropped her bomb, the plan was to evacuate, setting fire as they left. Her research would burn, leaving nothing for Julius to use. But they couldn't very well ignite the place if Gloria was left inside. Perhaps Flint's disruption device would take care of the cameras and anything left the fire didn't burn. But Mary's vision had still shown flames.

A sound behind her made her look.

Gloria was out of her bed and ripping the intravenous tubing from her arm. She swayed from side to side, but steadied herself on the bed. She jutted her chin out and avoided Mary's gaze, then walked, one shaky foot in front of the other.

"Get back in bed, Gloria." Mary made her way back to Gloria, but Gloria detoured to her desk. She rummaged through the drawer to pull something out: a bottle of Ethanol and a lighter. She poured the flammable liquid onto her desk, and the alcoholic stench filled the air. "I won't let him get this. It's not for him. You can take my laptop. Everything you need for the future is in there. One day the children will be smart enough to decipher it."

Then she set the desk on fire.

"Gloria!" Mary shouted. She raced to the bassinet to retrieve the baby and tucked him into her arms. Thankfully, the boy was asleep. "What are you doing?"

"What I should've done a long time ago." Gloria moved faster than Mary thought possible. She unlocked the door to the children's living quarters and pushed through, spraying the flammable liquid on the floor, on the walls, everywhere but the children's beds.

Sweet Mother.

"Out!" Gloria cried. "Everyone out!"

Mary raced in after her. Sister Josephine shot out of her seat, her knitting scattered to the floor. She held her palms in front of her in surrender.

"Dear Gloria, what are you doing?" Sister Josephine asked.

Gloria's eyes were wild as she picked up a metal cup from the kitchenette and used it to bang loudly on the mirrored window. A horrendous clatter filled the room, waking the children. Some of them cried, others shot out of bed. Then Gloria went to the wall, opened a hidden panel and pulled the Fire Alarm lever, alerting anyone left in the building.

Mary and Sister Josephine ushered the eldest children, Pride, Despair, and Wrath to stand near the door before going back for the younger children. Mary handed the newborn to the eldest, Pride, and told him to wait by the lab exit. The boy was tall. Only seven years old and coming up to her shoulder. Unlike his siblings who had darker hair like their mother, his long russet hair was thick and tarnished, almost like a lion's mane. But he refused to cut it. He took Envy without a word of complaint and went through to the laboratory. It would all be so new for them. They'd never been outside their living quarters.

"*Out.* Out children. There is a fire. Through this door." Mary peered through the laboratory and saw the secure exit door opening. Two unknown guards came rushing in and stopped dead in their tracks at the sight of children running toward them. "Take the baby," Mary shouted.

"And this one," Sister Josephine rushed down with the one-year-old girl in her arms. Sloth. Then the Sister rushed back to retrieve the two-year-old toddler, Gluttony, who woke screaming in fear and sucking his thumb between wails. Mary took hold of four-year-old Lust's hand, then collected the three-year-old boy Greed. Mary hefted him out of his bed and balanced him on her hip. Now, where was Gloria?

She was gone.

TEN

FLINT

THE MOMENT FLINT heard the fire alarm go off, he knew something had gone wrong.

Shit.

His thoughts flew to Mary. Those guards. Those fuck-tards. What if they hurt her? He pulled out his phone and tried to call, but she didn't pick up. He checked the security camera feed he'd hooked up to his phone and scrolled through locations until he viewed the floor they were on. No one was there yet.

He didn't want to hold up the lift in case they had to come down, so launched up the stairwell, two steps at a time. Sixteen floors later, his lungs burned and his heart beat rapidly, wanting to burst out of his chest. His thighs trembled with exertion. Thank God he ran miles a day, otherwise he'd not have made it. When he exited the stairwell, and ran into the reception lobby, he rolled his device along the floor and into the exposed lab area. Within ten minutes, all electrical devices would be wiped. All data on the computers, lost. He turned to the Project room and almost crashed into a security guard holding an infant.

"Fire," the guard bit out. "Stairs."

"The lift will be quicker," Flint said, nerves firing. He hit the down button on the elevator to call it to the level. "One trip down and you'll be safe. Go."

Flint didn't give the guard a chance to argue. When the door opened, he entered, hit the basement button, and then stood holding the doors open.

"Quick," Flint urged. "In the lift. Go." Another guard came rushing toward him with two children in tow. Despair, a tall girl with long hair clutched a small potted plant, and an auburn-haired boy... Flint couldn't remember their names. Behind him, the elder Sister jogged with a toddler in her arms, and dragged another running child.

He looked behind her and his heart skipped a beat. Mary came running with one child on her hip, and the other hand holding a girl, and a laptop tucked under her arm. They all filed into the elevator, filling up the small space. The infants cried and the guards had their hands full trying to console them.

Despair clutched her pot and wailed, "She's so sad. She's so sad."

A hand clutched at his shirt and tugged. He looked down to the teary eyes of Despair. She tugged again. "She's too sad. We have to help her."

"Where's Gloria?" he asked Mary and took the laptop from her arm.

Mary's eyes were bleak and empty, her expression shut down. When she spoke, it was cold and clipped. "I don't know."

An explosion erupted somewhere on the floor and they all flinched. A flare of heat hit their faces and the children screamed. The direction of the blast came from Barry's desk. All those specimen jars were flammable.

"What's happening, Mary?" he asked.

"She's burning everything," she replied. "We have to go. Now." With a fierce look, she punched the close door button. "Let go of the door, Flint."

"But..."

"Don't make this harder than it is." A look from Mary silenced him. He pulled his hand from the doors and they slid shut.

A shift of movement against Flint's side was the only warning he had before a little shadow burst past him and through the sliding doors, then they shut with a finality that had everyone silenced.

"No!" Flint slammed his fists on the doors, rattling the metal, again and again. "No!"

But there was no stopping the elevator's descent. Another explosion trembled the walls and an anguished cry ripped from Sister Josephine as she realized the same thing Flint had. Unable to let her suffer alone, Despair had run after her birth mother. In the space she had left was a potted bonsai plant, wobbling as the elevator moved. Flint looked to Mary, but she was a stone statue.

"Seven," she muttered. "I saw only seven children make it."

"I'll go back for her," Flint growled. "When we get to ground, I'll go back up the stairs."

Mary didn't respond. She kept her eyes to the floor, sucking air through her nose, and exhaling through her mouth.

Looking around wildly, Flint weighed his options. Stopping the lift would only jeopardize the rest. He had to go back up the stairs once they hit the bottom. Christ, his legs were jelly already, but he had to go back for the girl. He couldn't live with his negligence causing more death. Not again. Not after his friend and the accident.

The elevator pinged, signaling they were at basement level.

The doors opened. Flint picked up the plant and rushed out. "Van's over there."

He'd parked right up front. As he approached, he slid open the rear door and strapped the child in his arms into the seat.

"What are you doing?" One of the guards said.

"Getting these children to safety," Mary replied and relieved the man of the baby. She clipped him into a baby seat then ushered Flint to help her get the rest into a seatbelt.

The security guard shared a concerned glance with his

partner. "I'm going to radio this in. This isn't procedure." With his hands now free, the guard twisted to speak into his shoulder mic.

The second guard's head swiveled from Mary to Flint, to an equally surprised Sister Josephine. Then he darted a glance at the lift. "I'm going back for the kid." He disappeared into the same stairwell Flint had climbed earlier.

"I'll go back for Despair," Flint said to her, in the privacy of the van. "Get to her before the guard."

"No," she replied. "These seven are our priority. The fewer guards here, the fewer I have to hurt for us to get away."

"But, Mary. You can't possibly—"

"Why are you wearing those black clothes, Sister?" The guard's voice elevated from outside. "I don't think these children should leave the compound. The boss wouldn't like that. Stop strapping them in."

Mary shifted past Flint and got out of the van to respond. "It's not safe here. You saw what happened up there. If they've survived, it would be a miracle."

When Flint went over the plan in his head that day, it had not gone like this. It had been a series of reactions, prompted by well thought out actions. Zeros and ones. If this... then that. Logic. That was the way of programming. That was how things should go.

But this was not ordered. It was chaos.

Flint secured the last strap on the child and gave him a bottle he had waiting on the seat. He handed the smaller girl her toy cat and the bag of toys to the eldest to distribute. He gave the potted bonsai to the boy with long, auburn hair.

The eldest children did their best to console the youngest, each pitching in to help. They were a tight knit family. His chest clenched at the missing child, and he hoped, in his heart, that she had saved herself. Perhaps she'd crawled into the shelter of a cupboard or something.

He pulled out his cell and checked the camera feed from upstairs. They had shorted out, just like he'd planned. For once he wished that his gadgets didn't work. He took a deep breath, closed his eyes and counted to ten. He had to trust Mary.

Flint got out of the car and gestured for Sister Josephine to stand to the side with him. "We'll take it from here," he said to her quietly. "The Hildegard Sisterhood have everything planned."

Her eyes widened.

"Your colleague over there is... what is the word she used—"

"A Sinner," the sister whispered, nodding emphatically. "I can tell from her uniform."

Flint blinked. "You know?"

"Everyone in the Sisterhood knows about the Sinners. We don't know exactly who they are or what they do, but we understand they exist. They sacrifice their souls so the rest of us may flourish. Anything you need, I'll do."

"Why don't you go out the exit ramp and wait for the

Fire Department on the street. They'll need someone to brief them. Minus the sinner business." The word left a bad taste in Flint's mouth. She wasn't a sinner. Not to him. She was a hero. A saint.

"Of course." The Sister left, giving Mary a curt nod of respect as she passed.

Flint met Mary where she stood near the guard at the end of the van. She straightened herself. It was the first chance Flint had to closely inspect her Sinner uniform. Black, sleek, stretchy. Dark hair braided. Fists strapped like a boxer. Made for action. Made for silent nights, and dark things. Except the slash of red at her throat—the scarf pulled down over her neck. That was a promise of death.

But it was more than the uniform. A change had come over Mary. The soft, sexy, cheeky women he'd fallen for over the past two years was replaced with a cold, hard lethal weapon. Eyes full of danger watched the remaining guard.

The sound of screeching tires echoed in the parking garage. Lights flashed in the darkened area. Two black SUVs sped toward them.

While the guard inspected the approaching vehicles, Mary quietly lifted her red scarf to cover her mouth and nose. She turned to Flint.

A simple look, that's all that passed between them, and his heart almost surged out of his chest. Something was about to happen. Something dangerous. Deadly.

Mary closed the rear sliding door on the van. "Get in the car, Flint. Start the engine."

Shit. Fuck.

His blood turned cold, but he trusted Mary. He opened the driver side door.

"Step away from the vehicle," the guard said, unclipping his gun. He pointed the barrel at Flint, but his wary eyes darted to Mary, latching onto her new face scarf.

"You will not shoot with children in the van," Mary said, voice muffled through the fabric.

"I know how to aim, ma'am. I can take you out without hurting them."

The SUVs pulled to a stop, and an army of soldiers jumped out.

"Flint," Mary repeated, never taking her eyes off the guard. "Get in the car."

He hesitated. There were so many guns.

"Now," she barked.

ELEVEN

MARY

MARY SHUT the door behind Flint and faced the closest guard.

He lifted his gun and pointed it at her head. "I mean it, I'll shoot."

The blood pounding in Mary's ears drowned out all sound, and she forced herself to calm. Peace. Gather. Assess. Prepare. She heard her breath. Her heart. The snick of his metallic weapon, and then she entered the zone.

Time slowed.

She flicked her wrist. A dagger unsheathed from within her sleeve. A glint flashed in the air, and the knife was embedded in the guard's neck before he could blink. He dropped, the gun went off. Plaster on the roof sprayed white dust, making the air murky.

Perfect cover.

She zipped to his side, retrieved her knife, ignored the gurgling and blood.

Under the cloud of dust, Mary ducked behind a support pillar and pulled her second knife from her right sleeve. She flipped the blades in her palms as she centered herself.

Her breath. Her heart. Listen.

Mary closed her eyes and concentrated. Where were they?

A boot scuffle. A man's low voice. The crackle of a shoulder mic.

She rolled the daggers around her fingers and caught them in her palms. The blades were dull at the edges, but sharp at the points. Perfect for throwing and piercing.

There.

Mary released at two approaching shadows emerging from the dust. She ran forward, watching as the blades hit their mark in the center of their necks. They went down gurgling and gasping for air.

Six to go.

She continued, darting past the felled soldiers, yanking the knives out by the handle loops. Refocus. Retarget. To the right... and thirty degrees to the left. She threw.

Whoosh. Thud, thud.

Two more down. Four left.

A quick assessment showed the throwing knives were too far to retrieve. For a moment, she wished for her sword

—a perfectly balanced Katana gifted from the *Onna Bugeisha*. It was in the van. Also too far.

The remaining guards watched their comrades fall, but then their weapons were up. Assault rifles. Mass destruction in a small space.

So was she.

"You shoot, you risk the children," she shouted as she crouched and released small knives from straps at her ankles. She slid them between her fingers so three blades poked through each hand like claws growing from her knuckles.

They zeroed in on her position.

They aimed. Fired. *Crack! Crack!*

Mary twisted and ducked behind a support pillar. Bullets whizzed by, bursting the brick mortar, sending another cloud of dust into the air. A stinging pain sliced her right shoulder blade, and she hissed. Debris or bullet. She tested her arm by rotating. It burned, but she'd live.

They fired again and the white cloud of plaster bloomed, making her mouth dry when she breathed. Every time they did that, they gave her cover in the dust. She had to hurry. Creeping quickly, stealthily through the white bloom, she slipped to the next pillar, then the next. She crouched low. They hadn't seen her move and still trained their weapons on the spot she'd vacated, waiting, converging.

She darted toward their cars and, as quietly as she

could, punched the rear wheels with her bladed fists until
air hissed out.

They should've checked behind them, because she was
on them before they knew it.

She was a dark tornado, whirling and dominating. She
slashed the closest guard across the neck, twirled, then
sliced the second above the eyes, blinding him with his own
blood. Then she punched him. Hard. The blades pierced.
Hand to hand combat was sloppy, but she was angry. Furi-
ous. They were bulls in a china shop, discharging their
weapons like their surroundings didn't matter. Like the
children didn't matter.

They mattered.

She clenched her fist and hit him in the neck, piercing
skin and breaking cartilage. The man's scream bubbled. He
let go of his rifle to protect his face. She gripped the falling
weapon, spun and with two shots hit the final two guards in
the chest.

This all happened before the final crumb of plaster hit
the floor.

Mary paused, listening; breath quiet, heart loud. No
more guards, but a car coming.

She dropped the rifle, ran to the van, snapped the door
open and hopped in.

"Go!" she cried and hit the dash, ignoring Flint's horri-
fied face as he stepped on the gas.

DUST AND BLOOD COVERED MARY, but not as much as she'd feared. After wiping her hands and face with a baby wipe, she felt semi-decent.

They drove quietly for forty minutes before Flint attempted to speak. He'd opened his mouth a few times, but clicked his jaw shut. He shook his head, checked on the kids behind him and mumbled to himself, deep voice rumbling through the car.

The van descended into silence, nothing but the sound of tires whizzing, and air pushing on the windows. The children were asleep. It took twenty minutes for them to relax, but the drag of night and the soothing motion of travel wore them down until the last of them drifted off.

It had been just Flint and Mary for a few miles, and yet he'd said nothing.

Heat warmed Mary's face. She didn't know what to say. What did he think of her now? That look when she'd entered the car. His skin had turned pale. His pupils so black and big they covered his irises. He saw her kill and maim those men. It was necessary. It was also necessary to leave a woman and child behind in a burning building.

He must hate her.

Despite the loss, and the gaping void she feared would never close, she had no tears. No pain. She was numb. This was her. This violence was part of Mary. For years she'd been taught that it was a necessary evil, but only after Flint she understood that her life could be more. And she wanted that.

She wanted to feel again, just like she had when they'd kissed.

Suddenly, she was a little *bruja* girl back at a festival. Behind the performance tent her father had whipped her while her mother watched, sneering. How she hated her parents then. How she had wished to maim and torture them back. Mary's little back had bled and oozed from welts for days after that. All because earlier that morning, Mary had been so hungry, so starving out of her mind, that she hadn't paid attention to the vision she had earlier. Food was how they paid Mary, and they'd fed her nothing since the night before. She'd been so caught up with the taste of lunch that her mouth watered and her stomach cramped. Pictures of barbecued chicken swam before her eyes. The smell. The taste. When a man came and asked what his future held, her mind was elsewhere. She couldn't future-tell on demand, but had to remember what she'd seen in the days before, and try to relate it to the right customers. The memory was hard to force, and it demanded a lot of attention to detail.

In the end, someone had died. She couldn't remember who, but they all blamed her. If she was worth her money, she'd have seen how to stop it, how to prevent it.

A death. You couldn't come back from a death.

The hate for her parents still drove Mary to violence. She'd often wished they weren't hers, that they'd stolen her from loving, kind parents who would have fed her big family meals, who would have tucked her into a warm bed, and who would have kissed and cuddled her when she scraped her knee. But they weren't. They didn't feed her for days after that death... until she had grown too faint to walk.

Mary squeezed her eyes shut and tried to block out the memory, but it was replaced with a more recent failure. She'd done it again. Too caught up in her own feelings. If only she had written down her vision, like the Sisterhood had taught her, she would have noticed Gloria was missing. She would have noticed the seven children included the new baby, but not Despair. She would have seen past her hormones and starry eyes, and maybe she could have saved them.

Pain flared in her chest, expanding, threatening to block her airways.

She bit her lip and tried to glimpse Flint as the passing street lights illuminated his face. He had become impassive. Deathly quiet.

She should never have dragged him into this. He'd seen her kill without mercy, and she'd forced him to leave a child behind. Maybe it was better she sent the children to the Sisterhood, despite her promise to Gloria.

You couldn't come back from a death.

TWELVE

FLINT

FLINT WAS SO FAR out of his league he couldn't think. The police sirens blaring on the other side of the street didn't help. *Not after us.* They were fine. They'd escaped. He didn't even know where he was driving. He just drove. Away would be good. Another fucking country better.

What he'd witnessed had left him paralyzed with fear.

Those soldiers discharged their weapons without considering the children in the van. They were so goddamned lucky that not a single bullet pierced the metal walls of the vehicle. He'd almost had a heart attack when the first gun had fired. If it weren't for Mary—

His brain emptied.

Mary.

Fuck.

Fucking Super Woman that's who.

Christ. He scrubbed his face and blew air through his

nose. The shakes still wracked his body, aftershocks of adrenaline sporadically firing his nerve endings, lighting them up with nowhere to go. He was seriously jacked. He did not understand how she was so calm. Years of training, she'd said. Training as what? A mother-fucking-ninja? His fists tightened around the steering wheel, making his knuckles blanch. His foot tapped the floor. A quick check in the rearview showed the kids sleeping. They'd survived. More resilient than him.

It was okay. The kids were okay. Well, most of them were okay.

Shit.

Not okay. He rolled down the window and breathed the cold fresh air lest he vomit.

For the past forty minutes, he'd recounted the events in his head, seeing if he could come up with a different scenario, one where Gloria and the girl survived... but he couldn't. He slammed his fist on the steering wheel, making Mary jolt.

He knew deep down there was no way they could have gone back for Gloria and Despair and save the rest of children at the same time. The guards were there.

Sure, Mary knew some serious Mission Impossible shit... he gulped—he had a flash of blood spraying, a guard's artery being hit—he squeezed his eyes shut and forced the macabre image away, then opened to watch the road whiz by in the dark.

His fingers twisted on the wheel, making the leather

squeak. He didn't know what to think. They had had guns. They had fired. It was the only thing Mary could have done.

It was them, or us.

It was a miracle none of them had been hit.

He glanced at her and caught a snapshot of her profile, dark and brooding against the flashes of street light through the passenger window. The wind from his window whipped her hair around. She was so beautiful in that moment. So strong. So calm. She had single-handedly saved their fucking lives. He wanted to pull the van over, drag her from the car and kiss her senseless. He was in awe.

Flint rolled up his window.

Mary leaned forward to check the side mirror with a flicker of a frown, then settled back in her seat. Flint kept darting his gaze to watch her. Her arched black brows, her cute nose, full lips. A graceful neck that led down to... his gaze darted from her collarbone and over her shoulder to a blood stain on the back seat. She'd been hit. Blood oozed from a spot on her shoulder. He hadn't noticed before because of her red neck scarf.

"Mary, you've been shot," he said, breath hitching.

She didn't respond.

"Mary."

"It's just a graze," she mumbled vacantly.

Maybe she was in shock. The woman had just bled for them. The least he could do was see to her injuries, see about getting these kids to a safe place. Then he could figure out what the fuck he was doing next.

"Right. I'm stopping at a motel. It's late."

An odd look flickered over her face. For a minute, Flint thought she would not respond, but then she nodded. "A motel is a good idea. The abbey is too far to reach tonight."

Ten minutes later, Flint pulled the van into the parking lot of a faded highway motel just off the expressway. It was the first one they'd found. The sign flickered and was missing a letter, but the lot was clean and half full. He hoped that was a good sign. More patrons either meant decent motel, or druggies and undesirables. They needed a place to crash for the rest of the night and recoup. He parked the van and paid for their largest twin share room with cash, making their stay untraceable.

The room wasn't huge, but clean and private. Maroon curtains blocked the windows. The walls were mustard, and the paper peeled in places, but there was a TV, a bar fridge, a microwave and a small dining table. A modest couch lined a wall, and there was a bathroom behind a door. Two big quilted beds sat side by side. He pushed them together. It would be big enough for the kids to sleep on. There was a bassinet buggy in the van for the newborn. Mary could take the couch, Flint would sleep on the floor. He'd go out for extra blankets as soon as they settled. It wasn't great, but it would do for a few hours.

With a solid plan in his head, he felt better. Less chaotic.

Stealthily, they unbuckled the children one by one from the car and placed them on the beds. It was hard not to watch the children's faces as they slept. Warmth rushed his chest when two of the younger children cuddled each other like stuffed toys. Another clutched his shirt like he were a lifeline and a fierce surge of protection overcame him. Awestruck at their innocence, he thought, for once in his life he'd done good. *They'd* done good. He had to put aside his guilt for the one who didn't make it and focus on the seven that were saved.

Because of him and Mary, seven children would have a better life.

They would have a life, period.

Mary heated formula and fed the newborn with a look of wonder as she nursed the infant back to sleep.

Flint smiled. He'd been right when he told her she wasn't capable of killing children. Just seeing the way she gently handled the baby reinforced that. She was still wounded, but put the child's needs before her own, and in his eyes, that made her the best mother they could have. He was glad she'd be in their lives.

He settled the rest of their belongings inside, but kept one eye on Mary. The stone soldier had dissipated, and he caught her humming as she paced the length of the floor in front of the beds, quietly patting the baby in her arms. When she didn't think Flint was watching, she buried her face in the baby's neck and inhaled deeply. Her eyes were glistening when she pulled away, and then checked on each of the sleeping children, tucking them in tightly with one hand. She'd removed the boxing-tape from her hands while in the van. He noticed her knuckles then. They were purple and bruised.

He pursed his lips and, to Mary's surprise, he took the baby out of her arms. Envy was asleep, milk drunk and snoring softly. It was so adorable that Flint almost kept rocking the baby in his arms.

"How do they do that?" he whispered.

"Do what?" she replied, touching Envy's chin.

"Entrap you, just by being there. I can't stop looking at him."

"Because they are special. Important. They are the hope of the world."

Mary met his gaze and, for a moment, they shared an inescapable connection. The Mary he loved was in there, then her expression shuttered as though she were trying to protect her heart. But he'd seen it. He'd seen the love she was capable of.

He placed the baby gently in the bassinet and then guided Mary into the small bathroom. She still looked shocked as he shut the door behind them.

The room was tiny. A white bath with a shower and a floral curtain. White toilet. Single white vanity with a counter on either side of the basin and a mirror over it. Nothing special, but clean with fresh towels. He slipped a hand towel off the rack and turned the faucet. Once the towel was wet, he wrung it out.

"All right. Let's see that wound."

Mary flinched. "I can sort myself out. In fact, your job is done. You've been paid, you can leave now. I can get them to the Sisterhood myself. Thank you."

She took the wet towel out of his hands and turned to the mirror to see her wound. He stood behind her, watching her reflection ignore him.

The fuck?

Everything got real quiet. No sounds except the drip of the faucet and their soft steady breathing.

"Have I done something wrong?" Flint asked quietly, catching her eyes in the mirror.

The haggard look she returned sent all sorts of mixed messages running through his body. She'd shut down. Or had he really been part of the mission all along?

No. He refused to believe that. Their kiss had told him otherwise.

She'd told him once that her parents didn't want her, that she was an orphan. He wasn't going to quit on her like her parents. "Mary."

"I saw the look you gave me in the car, Flint. That's okay. I'm not sorry about what I did to save those children. I'm not sorry I asked you to leave Biolum Industries with me." She inhaled deeply, broke eye contact and craned her neck to view her shoulder wound. She tried prying the frayed fabric away.

Good luck with that. The wound was behind two layers of clothing. A shirt and a woolen vest. He arched an eyebrow. She wanted to play woe is me, then fine. He'd watch her squirm.

"And exactly how was it that I looked at you, because, unless it's with awe, then it's news to me." He folded his arms.

Her eyes widened, lashes lifting to expose stunning dark irises, then she glanced down at her shirt. "Do you mind? I have to undress."

"So undress."

He enjoyed the blush staining her cheeks despite the irritation swimming in her eyes. Didn't matter. That dull, distant woman he'd driven here was gone. From the moment she'd smelled the baby's sweet scent of innocence, Mary had returned to him. Flint had seen her physically unwind, the tension leaving her shoulders, the frown lines smooth from her face. Her love had been there before she'd locked it away, and he was determined to bring it back.

"You're just going to stand there?" she asked.

"We both know you're not a nun, Mary, so quit it with the modesty. Just let me help you."

She ground her teeth. "Fine."

Her hands lifted to the back of her neck to grip the collar of her vest, intending to pull over her head... but winced. The wince turned into a grimace, she froze and squeezed her eyes shut. A tear glistened at the corner of her lashes.

"Mary," Flint whispered. He stepped into her, pressing

his body against her back, capturing her wrists. "Let me help you."

"No," she said. Her words were harsh, but she weakened against his front. "Now's your chance. You should go. Leave and never come back."

He encircled her front and nuzzled her neck. "Why would I leave?"

"Because you didn't sign up for this. You didn't sign up for me. You don't even know who I am." Her eyes opened and met his in the mirror. Then she whirled on him so they were face to face, inches apart. "You have your money. It's what you wanted. You should go."

Anger rose inside him. "You think I'm only here for the money?"

She didn't answer.

"Jeez, woman. I can't tell if you're just blind or naïve."

She gasped. "You have the nerve to judge me? You're the one who signed up to pay for someone else's mistake."

"Fuck you, Mary, if you think that's why I'm here."

"Eight million dollars, Flint. Take it. Leave. It's one hell of a college fund."

"Shut up." He squeezed her arms. Goddamn that woman. Cheap shot, hitting him where it hurt, but he didn't buy it. Screw her words. "You'll have to physically remove me if you want me to leave."

Her entire body relaxed, softened like jelly, as though she'd been holding it together by sheer will. And now it was gone. When she spoke, her voice was strained. "Before you came along, my visions always showed everyone else surviving. For months I saw the same thing, then it all changed after our moment in the elevator."

"Are you blaming this on me now?" Fine. He'd let her do that if it helped her sleep tonight. He could take it. What was one more fuck up if he had her in his arms?

Mary's hands fisted his shirt, her eyes pleaded with him, helpless. "I'm blaming this on *me*. If I wasn't so wrapped up in my selfish desires, I would've noticed the other changes in the vision." An anguished cry ripped from her. "I allowed myself to want something, and the vision changed! Don't you see? It's my fault! My fault they're dead."

Flint yanked her to his chest and held her close. She resisted at first, then melted into him until their bodies forged a new shape. She knew it. Her body knew it. They fit.

"Shh." He tightened his grip. She felt so good in his arms. Small but powerful, and she needed him. "This is not your fault."

"It is, it is." She sobbed, crying into his chest, tears soaking his shirt.

"Because I want you? Because you want me?"

"Yes. I got distracted. Lost sight of the mission."

"Mary," he said, deadly serious. "There's one flaw in your logic. You're assuming this all changed that day in the lift, but—Mary, look at me." He hooked a finger under her chin to lift her gaze. "I've wanted you since I first met you.

Fuck. I wanted you so bad, I thought I was going to hell right then and there. You think you have a choice in this, but you got me. There's no going back. I'm not letting go. Never."

But she kept shaking her head.

"Think about it differently," he continued. "What if, with Julius' new demand, everything changed? What if that horrible second future you saw was coming true, and you and me together is the only thing in its way?"

Mary stilled. Her eyes widened. "That's what Gloria said."

"It is?"

"Yes, she said we were stronger together."

"Gloria was a smart lady."

Still dumbfounded, Mary could only nod. There was something more there, something Mary couldn't share yet, but Flint knew he'd get it out of her eventually.

"Mary, there are so many variables. And, yes, we lost a few people on the way and it will cut us up for the rest of our lives, but you know what? We fucking did our best, Mary. We stood up and took action when no one else did. Those kids have a chance at a real life now."

She pulled away, arching her head back, catching his eyes.

"You and me," she whispered. "Together."

"Yeah." He cupped her face, thumb wiping the tear from her cheek. "God, you're beautiful."

He leaned in to kiss her, but stopped. He hadn't

noticed before because her hair was dark, but around her ear there was dried blood. "And filthy."

Doubt flickered in her eyes, but before she could hold onto her thoughts, he'd switched on the shower. In seconds, steam filled the room, and he helped her out of her woolen vest.

"C'mon. Let's get you out of this, get you washed, check your wound and..." He lost focus. Mary had unbuttoned her shirt, and it gaped open, exposing two perfect mounds of flesh curving over a simple black bra. Her chest rose and fell with her quickening breath. He couldn't stop staring. He'd dreamed about those breasts. He'd fantasized about them. Nightly. In the shower. In his bed. In the elevator. Behind her in the line at the coffee counter in the staff break room. And now they were here, inches away from him. All he had to do was reach out...

Flint swallowed hard. Licked his lips. Met her uncertain eyes.

She was nervous, anxious... hopeful.

He'd never save the world like she would, but he could be her hero. He could wash her, clean her, hold her... make her forget. He lifted his finger to hook on her collar and slid her shirt off.

THIRTEEN

MARY

MARY WATCHED Flint as he reverently undressed her. Her ears burned. Her heart pounded. Her eyes and throat were raw from crying. She was done with feeling guilty for wanting. This—what they had between them—was special. This was how she came back from death. This was how she lived again.

Gloria was right. Love had a way of bringing out the best in people.

Flint was also right. Anything could have made her original vision change course. It could have been a decision someone else made, not her. And after she'd admonished him for paying for someone else's mistake, she'd almost done the same thing.

Not anymore.

If she wanted a world full of love, she had to lead by example. Starting right now. Mary pulled the shower curtain back and stepped into the hot stream and let it wash away her anxiety. The water pulsed down on her face, her back, her chest. Two seconds later, she realized Flint hadn't followed her. Mary turned around, her body left the spray, and she shivered, goosebumps erupting over her skin.

Flint's gaze snagged on her mouth, then traveled down... and back up. He watched her, mesmerized.

"Are you going to help me?" she asked.

"I'm going to do more than help you," he said, voice raw. "I'm going to make you forget everything that made you cry."

"And how are you going to do that?"

"I'm going to run my fingers all over your soapy body, starting with your shoulders, your beautiful neck, and then work my way down to your breasts. Then I'm going to take each nipple into my mouth and suck on them until you beg me to stop."

A slow, sinful smile curved his lips.

"While my mouth is doing that," he continued, eyes roving where his words indicated, "my fingers will slide downward, over your stomach, your perfect ass, between your legs... and then I'm going to do things that will have you moaning my name. I might even—"

"Are you going to talk about it, or do it?"

"Fuck." He pulled his shirt over his head and threw it to the floor with earnest. "I'm going to do it."

The rest of his clothes were gone in a blink and he crowded into the shower, taking up the small space with his big body. She barely had time to enjoy the view of his lean torso before he was on her. His fingers slotted into her wet hair, his thumbs pressed against her cheeks and he kissed her. *Sweet heaven*, he tasted good, and it drove her wild. She licked him back, nipped his lip, tasted his sweet salty tang, believing every minute of his words. He'd make her forget the bad and replace it with good.

The stiffness in her shoulder, the ache in her knuckles, all were taken over by sparks of pleasure zipping through her body. Aftershocks. Fireworks. Her hands landed on his chest, slipped down his pecs, abs, and traveled further south. He shuddered, skin pulling taut under her touch.

"Mary," he whispered hotly into her mouth, warning her. He pulled away, eyes dreamy and dazed. "I said I would wash you. Shit. Where's the fucking soap?"

Mary chuckled. "There." She pointed.

"Good. Fucking great." He picked up the fresh bar from the dish, unwrapped the paper and wantonly ditched the trash over the curtain. With a salacious wiggle of his eyebrows, he lathered it between his hands. "I'm going to wash the fuck out of you. Just watch me. No. Scratch that. Don't watch me. Turn around. I can't concentrate when you look at me that way."

Mary couldn't help laughing, her mood lifting. She turned to face the faucet, her back to Flint, wondering how the hell he kept doing that—cheering her up. He always did, no matter what. Even if he cursed, teased her, challenged her, his incorrigible energy was all she needed to brighten a stormy day. She pressed her palms to the wall for balance and closed her eyes.

Two warm, slippery hands landed on her neck, lathered in circles, and then slid up into her hair, washing and massaging. Then he slid and slipped down over her collarbone to her front. Further. He glided to her breasts and took special attention. Hot fingers kneaded and massaged, slipping up the underside, grazing over her nipples, skimming to her neck and then down again. And up again. *Lord* she would burst with need. Slowly, surely every nerve ending tightened in her body. Hot lips landed on the spot under her ear. His tongue darted out and tasted her flesh.

She moaned and pushed back. The cushion of her rear hit his erection, and he hissed in a breath. He splayed his fingers on her stomach and tugged her tighter, pressing his shaft against the small of her back, groaning. His voice rumbled up her spine in the most delicious way. Then he pulled back, picked up the soap, reloaded and turned her around to face him, determined. Yep. He wanted to wash her. He was going to do it right.

"Your wound looks okay," he murmured.

"Is there bone showing?" she asked.

He shook his head.

"Good," she breathed. "Need stitches?"

Another shake of the head. "I don't think so. Bleeding's stopped."

His cheeks flushed, his dark hair peppered with droplets of water that fell to his face and beard. His brows drew together in concentration. And then he reached around her shoulders and rubbed her back, taking special care over her bullet graze. After he was done, he stepped closer, slotting himself between her legs, teasing her, rocking his shaft gently back and forward. He feathered his fingers down her spine, delighting in the feel of her body, watching her come undone before his eyes.

Mary's breath came fast, her legs weakened. She wanted to reach out and take him in her hands, to guide him inside her, but he pushed her away and urged her to hold onto his waist. He braced his hands behind her back and arched her backward. Bending low, he captured a stiff nipple in his mouth and rolled it with his tongue.

Bliss exploded in her body.

"More." Mary moaned again, arching back further. "Harder."

He flicked her nipple with his tongue and desire arrowed straight down between her legs, making her gasp.

"Flint," she breathed, trying to take him in her hands again. "Now."

"Now what?" he smiled against her skin.

She dug her hips into him, which only made his smile widen. He kissed his way back to her mouth, tongue dueling with hers. Mary gave back, deepening their kiss, losing herself, hands speared into his hair. "Now more."

"Now this?" His fingers trailed down her stomach and slipped between her legs. He applied pressure to her most sensitive spot, setting off an explosion of need.

"Or now this?" He delved lower and slid a finger inside her, unleashing a fresh torrent of desire.

Her nails clawed his back. "Yes. More. Stop teasing. I can't..."

"Or now this?" Flint's voice dropped to baritone, deep, scratchy and velvet-like.

Then he dropped to his knees and pressed his face into her stomach. He licked the water running down her body, circled her belly button and went lower.

"Sweet Mother," she whispered as his tongue reached between her legs, pushing between her folds. His touch was like nothing she'd ever felt before, so sure, so sensual. *This*—all this feeling—she felt so alive. How could she ever believe otherwise?

She fisted his hair and tugged him closer. Her head lolled to the side, rolling on the tiles. "Flint..." she moaned and rocked her hips against his face, trying to get him to go faster, harder.

He lifted her leg and draped it over his shoulder. He focused his tongue on her sensitive nub, worked her relentlessly, then buried his tongue deep inside. Heat coiled in her belly, pulling everything tight until waves of ecstasy crashed into her and she threw her head back, biting her lip to stop herself from screaming his name.

Mary stared at the curtains, watching the floral pattern spin around her as she slowly came back to herself. The water fell in a rhythmic pulse, filtering away into the drain, taking with it her inhibitions, her hesitations. Her entire body trembled as Flint tasted his way back up her body, fingers sliding confidently up her sides. She lifted his face to her lips and kissed him languidly.

He moved to turn the faucet off.

"What are you doing?" she asked, voice trembling. "We're not done yet."

Flint pulled back so he could look her in the eyes. "Mary, I... didn't bring protection. I didn't exactly expect to be doing this."

"Protection. You mean condoms?"

"Yes. I'm clean, I mean... I haven't been with another person in a long time and I've been tested—"

"I'm barren," she whispered.

"What?"

Heat surged to her cheeks at the embarrassment. "I'm sorry if that will be a problem for you, for us, but I can't have children. The nuns think it might have had something to do with me starving for half my childhood, but it could also be the years of rigorous training. I just don't know."

Horror danced over his features, then anger flashed in his eyes. "You starved for half your childhood? Or the training the Sisterhood gave you? Who in their right mind would treat a child that way?"

"There's a lot of sin in this world. A lot of bad people." She couldn't look at him. "Like me."

"No. I don't believe for an instance what they call you. You're not a sinner. You're a saint." Flint buried his face in her neck. "Please believe me when I say, you're so very special to me. Please believe that. I'm so sorry that happened to you."

"I'm fine now," Mary said.

"But once you weren't, and the Sisterhood took advantage of a broken child. It's wrong. I won't let them do that to these children. I love you, Mary. All of you."

"I love you too," she whispered. Tears stung her eyes, and she hugged him tighter. She felt so secure, so warm and safe in his strong arms. He made her feel good, like everything would always be okay. He wanted her. Always. She never wanted it to end. She hoped it didn't have to. "And... I'm better than fine. In fact..." Mary slid her hand down between their bodies and took hold of his shaft, still firm. She stroked.

A low groan escaped his throat.

"Now?" she asked, smiling playfully.

"Heck yeah." He bit down gently on her good shoulder, then twisted her around to face the wall again. "Put your hands on the tiles. Lean forward. Ass back. Yes. Shit. Like that."

The tip of his cock teased her entrance, and she cried out, everything inside winding tight again, simmering with heat. She couldn't wait anymore, couldn't explain it, but she needed that connection. She pressed back into him, filling herself with his length.

They both stilled, reveling in the sensation of fitting together, and then she pulled out and began a slow, deliberate rhythm until even Flint lost control. He quickened to harder, faster strokes, bringing her back to the brink until finally her thighs clenched and her body gripped him tighter as she tipped into oblivion, forgetting all the pain and heartache just like he promised.

"Shit," he growled and tensed, climaxing. He dropped his head between her shoulder blades, hugging her tight. "Oh Mary," he whispered. "You've got me now. I'm sorry, but I'm not sorry. I'm going to have to do that again tomorrow. And the next day. And the next. I'm never leaving you. I want you to feel loved for the rest of your life."

Mary took a moment to catch her breath before glancing at him over her shoulder, eyes filled with sass. "I won't let you make me wait until tomorrow."

FOURTEEN

FLINT

IT SEEMED like only seconds since Flint had laid down on the couch with Mary and closed his eyes, but he woke to the sound of a baby crying and empty arms. Sunlight illuminated the room through gaps in the curtains, leaving dust rays slicing over the beds.

The children were waking, prodding and poking anyone left asleep. Flint rubbed his eyes and looked for Mary. She stood in the bathroom with the newborn tucked into her arms, rocking him back and forth, quietly humming. She had replaced her ruined nun attire from the day before with a very normal, very casual outfit—jeans and T-shirt. Her long, black straight hair fanned about her shoulders and he had an urge to run his fingers through its silky length.

Flint's gaze traveled to Mary's face and his throat

closed up with emotion. The adoration in her eyes as she gazed down at the baby said it all. She cared as much for these children as if they were her own—except, she couldn't have her own. But instead of swearing off children, she faced her pain head on. The Sisterhood wanted her to infiltrate Biolum Industries and spirit the children away. But she did more than that. She nurtured them. Protected them. Loved them.

That woman was magnificent. For a moment, her brilliance overwhelmed him, and he was lost watching her. Before they'd fallen asleep last night, she'd confessed the truth of her past. She came from a shitty childhood where her parents used and abused her, and then she shifted to another kind of abuse, the Hildegard Sisterhood. A bad taste entered his mouth, and he took a moment to realize what it was. He didn't like them—the Sisterhood. He'd never met them, but he didn't like them. He didn't like the fact they'd picked up a starving child and persuaded her to train like a soldier for their cause. They'd convinced her she was a *sinner,* for Christ's sake. Years, decades, they manipulated her... enough to possibly make her barren. What would that do to the children?

The warmth in his heart turned to rock-hard resolve as a new plan formed in his head. He wouldn't ignore his gut instinct. This time, he'd do something about it.

"You have hair on your face!" came a tiny voice from his side.

It was the small girl, not the baby, but the... maybe four-year-old? She had on flannelette pajamas that had pictures of unicorns on them. Her hair was dark, wavy and came half way down to her back. She looked like a mini Gloria. Wild, pale and very clever.

"It's called a beard," he said and scratched his jaw. He must look like Big Foot to them.

Her eyes widened. "And your voice is funny. You have a funny voice."

He chuckled, but then wondered if she'd ever seen a grown man. They'd been locked up in that room for years, with only the nuns and other children as their companions. And now they were supposed to hand them over to more nuns.

"What's your name?" he asked.

She smiled. "Lust. What's yours?"

Flint flinched. "Yeah, I'm not calling you that. Don't you have a real name?"

"We only have one name. Mine's Wrath," said an older boy from the bed. He had short black hair that stuck up in a natural Mohawk. He jumped over his siblings as though they were an obstacle course, bounced near the toddler, and jumped back. "Why have two names?"

"Well, it's not so much having two names, just more appropriate names," Flint elaborated.

"What's applopliate?" said the little girl.

The tallest boy, who had been tickling the one-year-old

on the bed rolled his eyes. He had long, shaggy hair. He looked quite wild, yet his golden eyes were smart and shrewd. "It means fitting, Lust." Then he shot a glance Flint's way. "I'm Pride, by the way."

"Fitting. What's fitting?" she asked again.

"Aargh, you ask so many questions," Wrath burst out.

"*You* ask too many questions!" The little girl jumped on the bed then launched onto her big brother's back where she wrapped her hands around his face, blocking his sight.

"I hungry," cried a toddler the same time another child, possibly Greed, said, "Where's Sister Josephine?"

"Ahh..." Flint swallowed and glanced at Mary who, thankfully, walked back into the room. She lifted her brows and shrugged.

"Um," he continued. "I told Sister Josephine that the Hildegard Sisterhood would look after you from now on, and she knows you'll be in safe hands, so she left to check on emergency services."

"Who's the Hildegard Sisterhood? Where's 'Spair? She always makes me give her a morning cuddle." This was Lust again—*Christ*. He was not calling her that. Maybe something starting with the same letter as her sin... Lauren... Lizzy... Liza. Yeah, Liza was good. Easy to remember.

"Spare?" he asked. "Who's Spare?"

"She means Despair." Pride gave Flint a pained look as if to say, *You know all the answers? Answer that!*

Mary laid the sleeping infant down in his bassinet.

"Did you just say you told Sister Josephine about the Sisterhood?"

"Yes," Flint replied. "I'm sorry, was I not meant to? I thought she worked there too. After I spoke about you being the Sinner, Sister Josephine said she would do anything we asked."

She pursed her lips and cast a worried glance at the watchful children. "We'll talk more about this in a minute."

Flint could sense the discord rising in Mary, but she pushed it down until she helped the children. She unzipped and zipped bags in a frenzy, handing packets of snacks to the older children. Flint jumped in to help her, to pick fruit and distribute, but ended up feeling rather useless. She had everything sorted and she did it with a smile.

"Here's a snack, pumpkin," she said to Wrath then ruffled his hair. "You need to keep your energy up so you can grow big and strong."

"But I don't like it."

"Well, how about when we get to our forever home, I make you something special, like—"

"Like pancakes with maple bacon?" Wrath jumped on the bed, excited. "You promised us you would make it once."

"Oh my, you remembered? That was months ago."

Gluttony popped his thumb out of his mouth and showed her a toothless grin. "Pwease?"

Mary laughed and nodded. "Whatever you want. But

in the meantime, please can you all have a bar? I know it's not the best, but I'll promise we'll get something better soon."

Begrudgingly, the children did as they were told.

When she was done dishing out the protein bars, Mary took his hand and they slipped out the front door.

The fresh morning air gave Flint goosebumps, and Mary a pink nose. He was immediately reminded of what they did together last night, how she was flushed pink in the shower, how she tasted. God, he wanted to do it all again. Every goddamned night.

"I don't know what to do, Flint," she confessed. "I haven't had a vision about this."

"Okay, well, let's think it through," he said and picked up her hand to kiss her bruised knuckles. "First, you haven't kissed me good morning."

Her eyes widened, and the corner of her perfect mouth twitched.

He thought she would argue with him, but her gaze dropped to his lips and turned hungry. She slotted her fingers behind his neck, and he did the same to her. Slowly, as though they had all the time in the world, they pressed their lips together.

"Good morning," she said, smiling up at him.

And goddamn it, that smile went straight to his cock, rousing it. "Shit Mary," he said and tugged her close, burying his face into her soft, freshly washed hair. The soap scent from the night before connected with his body in a way that had everything inside him clench. "I can't wait to spend the rest of my life saying good morning to you."

That earned him another kiss on the lips.

Then she sighed. "I want that so bad. But first, we have to figure out what we're doing."

"Right. Right." He pulled back so he could focus because the feel of her soft yet firm body was too distracting. "Let me get on top of this. Did your old visions say to go to the Sisterhood?"

"Yes."

"And the new one?"

"The only thing the new vision showed was all of our faces, in this room."

"So as far as that could mean, no Sisterhood."

She didn't answer, just stared at him, considering. He couldn't read her expression. It was as though she waited for him to respond as though she wanted him to decide for her. Part of him believed it wasn't his responsibility, but the other part, the louder part, took him back to that day he let his friend drive home drunk. That morning he woke to the news of the accident had been the worst morning of his life. He'd been heartbroken, physically sick. To know he had the chance to stop it had almost done him in. The guilt still echoed loudly in his soul every time he saw a young child with her family.

The past day with Mary and the children had given him purpose again. He knew what he wanted to do, he just needed find out what she wanted to do.

"What do you want, Mary?"

"Me?"

"Yeah you. What does your gut tell you?"

"Well, I've been thinking, and Gloria said—"

"Forget what Gloria said."

"If you let me finish, Gloria said they have special abilities that will unlock once they meet their mate for life, and that these will help them fight the evil of their sin. Without a mate, they risk falling prey to the sin they fight."

"What are you saying?"

"I... I guess what I'm saying is that if we don't want that destructive future to eventuate, then they need love in their lives."

Flint looked at the hotel room. Those little kids inside... so innocent now, but not forever. Pride already seemed jaded.

Lust's little girly voice piped up inside the room. She had spunk that kid, and she was only four, maybe five.

He made his decision hours ago.

"We don't go," he said. "We take the kids off grid. We raise them ourselves. You're a fucking ninja, you can teach them how to protect themselves. I can teach them... well, how to build a robot, or some shit, but the point is, we might even give them a chance for a normal childhood. School. Fun. Friends."

"But... the Sisterhood."

"Fuck the Sisterhood. What have they done for you except suck your soul away? I don't like them, no offense. I know they saved you from your parents but, Mary, they used you. They wanted you to kill the children! They're as bad as the company that created them."

She said nothing for a while.

Flint licked his lips and kept going. "Mary, we lost their sister, but we don't have to lose them. You said they need love in their lives. We can provide that for them. You and me."

"Flint. That's a massive commitment. That's your entire life we're talking about. You only found out about them yesterday."

"But I fell in love with you two years ago."

"What?"

"Like I said last night, from the moment I laid eyes on you, I knew. Even though my mind said you weren't available, my heart was gone. I trust you. I'm with you, all the way. If you say these children need love in their lives, then let's give it to them. You're more than the Sisterhood. You're more than a *bruja*."

Tears welled in her brown eyes and her bottom lip trembled. She pulled his face to hers and kissed him, hard. When she pulled back, her eyes locked with his. "I love you so much. Let's do this. You, me, and the seven."

"Done. On one condition."

Fear flashed in her eyes. "What?"

"We give them real names."

Mary laughed. "And a new last name for us."

"You don't like Fydler?"

"I love it, but we must change our identities."

"Oh, of course. Okay, got any ideas?"

She thought about it for a moment, then a smile danced on her face. "How about Lazarus."

"Lazarus," he said, testing the name. "Laz-ar-us. Okay. Sounds good. Kinda like lazy-ass but, okay. We can work with it. Why that name?"

"Because he was the only other man in the bible apart from Jesus who came back from the dead." She turned serious on Flint. "You brought me back from death, Flint."

"Then Lazarus is perfect." He kissed her on the forehead.

A suspicious sound came from inside the room, as though a lamp had dropped.

Mary gave Flint a sideways glance. "Last chance to back out—take your money and run."

"Mary, this is a battle I'm prepared to fight. You got me until the end."

As they entered the motel room, Flint's foot knocked on something. A pebble. He picked it up with a smile and handed it to Mary.

"What's this for?" she asked.

"For our new collection."

"For a new garden," she whispered then tipped on her toes to kiss him on the cheek. "It's perfect."

THE END.

Thank you for reading *Sinner*.
Ready for more Deadly Seven? Jump right into the box set bargain where you can continue with get Envy and Greed.
Or read on for a three chapter preview.

ENVY EXCERPT

ONE

EVAN LAZARUS

HE WOKE IN A STRANGE PLACE.

Thick, pungent air dragged into his lungs from the darkness. His head pounded and his body ached to the point of pain. Soft and lumpy beneath him. Hard and cold at his sides. When he fumbled around, his movement stirred the rancid odor. He knew exactly where he was.

Dumpster.

And if he'd hidden in a Dumpster, he most likely wore his combat uniform—a quick pat down his leather pants and tug on his hood confirmed that. His hands came away sticky, and when he touched his thumb to his forefinger, the tackiness remained. He held it to his nose and sniffed. Sweet, metallic, thick: Blood.

But whose?

And, how did he get here?

Before panic set roots in his chest, he thought to

himself: *Evan Lazarus. Your name is Evan Lazarus. You fight the deadly sin envy. You save people.*

Sometimes.

Maybe.

He must have done something terrible... something worth hiding from. And rather than call for help, he'd hidden, because, why would the Deadly Seven help him? They were only his family.

Evan moved to lift the lid on the Dumpster, but a pain pierced his torso. The sensation brought memories of the previous night flashing in a dizzying torrent. Multiple pairs of hands forced him down. Fists slammed into his eye sockets and cheekbones. Blinding pain. Swollen vision. Boots pounded into his abdomen. Air wheezed from his lungs. A crow bar to his ribs, jaw, knees. He'd bucked hard, but they'd ruthlessly pinned him down, driving his limbs wider until pain screamed in his joints, leaving his torso vulnerable to more violence... then he'd yielded and smiled and laughed. Because he'd deserved it.

Evan scrubbed his face with his hand to wipe the memory, but the words of his assailant came hurtling back: *"If you're looking for validation, kid, you're in the wrong place. You should have thrown the fight like we told you to."* Then the lights had gone out.

Evan laid in the dark Dumpster, eyes closed, acutely aware of every ache and stab of pain in his body. They'd left him for dead.

But he wasn't dead.

Well, he couldn't stay there forever.

Taking a chance he pushed the lid open and let it crash against the wall. Sweet, crisp air burned his lungs and he almost choked on the freshness. Dawn peeked over the tall grungey cityscape, casting the alley walls into stark chiaroscuro. Any other day he might have been awed enough to paint the atmospheric sight, but today his mood was murky and heavy like the sky.

It would rain soon and, dammit, his fighting leathers chafed when wet. At least he'd left his weapons at home before he'd allowed himself to be a boxing bag at the fight ring the night before.

He searched for a plastic bag in the Dumpster then crawled out and peeled his jacket and mouth scarf off, leaving him in a used-to-be-white T-shirt and blood-stained leather pants.

Suddenly, the air rippled to his right, lighting his senses on fire. His arm shot out in time for a projectile to hit his palm, fingers snapping shut over the object within. A base-ball. From... he pushed his awareness out, searching for envy. There. To the right. The sense of deadly sin trickled toward him, wriggling in his gut like grimy feathered fingers, sparking an intense hunger to search and destroy. This supernatural sixth sense was something all his siblings had, except each sensed a different sin. If they didn't chase down the worst of sinners and eliminate or contain, then the sense would drive them insane.

Perhaps it already had.

There were a lot of sinners in Cardinal City.

A lot of envy.

He forced his urge to fight down. This particular sense of envy was small. Tiny. Not worth his time.

Children. Two of them.

Shit.

They might have seen him get out of his battle gear.

"Hey, nice catch, mister. Wish I was that good." A dirty little leaguer trotted over. Grime on his cheeks. Dirt on the cuffs of his jeans. Holes in his sneakers.

"Hey yourself, kid." Evan stuffed his jacket and scarf into the plastic bag, hiding evidence of his secret. "Go home. It's early."

So early. Or late. He couldn't decide. His dry throat begged for a drink. And an aspirin. Also a shower and then sleep and the sweet oblivion it brought. Josie would have to manage opening the tattoo shop on her own, his bed called to him.

Light flashed from the alley exit a few meters away as early morning commuters began their assault on the city. Evan turned in the opposite direction, intending to find a dark spot so he could hit the rooftops and trail the dying shadows home.

Fire-escape up ahead. Perfect.

As he walked, he blindly lobbed the ball over his shoulder. A cry of amazement proved he hit his mark as the kid caught it in his glove.

Envy from the children spiked three-fold, echoing in Evan's gut, and they ran after him, asking for an autograph.

Double shit.

"Why would you want an autograph?" he asked, testing the waters.

"Because you're one of *them!*"

Evan fisted his plastic bag. He paused. Turned.

The second boy was pale with wide blue eyes. Dark hair stuck up in the middle of his crown in a natural Mohawk or one hell of a cow-lick. Freckles hid behind his grubby cheeks. The first boy swam in an oversized Yankees jersey. Taller and similar facial structure to the second. Must be brothers. Yankee boy clutched the ball in his hand.

"One of who?" Evan asked.

"You know, the Deadly Seven." The smallest boy jumped around him like an eager grasshopper, spiky hair bouncing.

"You got the wrong idea, kid."

The eldest shot him a withering stare. "We're not stupid. Or blind—"

"Yeah, blind," chimed in the youngest.

"We saw you take your jacket off. *The* jacket." He wiggled his brows and eyed the plastic bag in Evan's hands.

Evan groaned and then took a deep breath while he decided how to handle them. Fuck it. They were only kids. Who would believe them? "Probably not a good idea. I'm not very popular at the moment."

"That's okay, Mr. Deadly sir, I like you."

Those three little words stabbed Evan in the heart.

"Well, that makes one of us." He continued to stroll toward the fire escape.

"C'mon, please?" The children jogged backwards in front of him, holding out the ball. "It will only take a minute. Wow. Is that blood? Did you catch some baddies?"

Only himself.

Evan stopped under the escape ladder and sighed. He shouldn't be talking with them, but it was nice to have anyone—even a couple of runts—have faith.

"Can you sign my baseball? *Please.*"

The Yankees kid smiled and threw his ball high above, intending to catch it in his glove to show off, but the round projectile hit the fire-escape instead. A loud clang sounded and the rusty retractable ladder dropped.

"Look out!" Evan shouted.

He shoved the boy out of the way only to have the broken ladder impale his own shoulder. He landed heavily on his knees and tried to breathe through the crippling agony, except the ladder pushed down and he was already drained and sore from the night before.

He heaved.

Pain splintered in his shoulder and black dots danced before his eyes. He almost lost sight.

He could do this. Especially in front of the kids. Fuck the night before. Screw the injuries he still recovered from. *C'mon, Evan. Do this.*

Squeezing his eyes shut, he gathered focus, and

breathed through the fog until ready. Gripping tight, he lifted the lance from his flesh. A wet, tearing sound made him cringe, but he heaved out of harm's way. Pain splintered the back of his head as he hit the brick wall, crumbling mortar and rock. A fresh wave of nausea rolled through him.

Perfect. He couldn't even save himself.

The sound of a small boy's voice broke through his agony. "Mason, he don't look so good."

"Yeah. Mr. Deadly, sir, are you okay?"

That was debatable. He tried to laugh, but a strangled sound came out.

You wouldn't see his siblings in this situation.

Evan flared his eyes to focus through the blur. He bit his lip and held his wrist in front of his face to view the Yin-Yang tattoo. The bio-indicated ink itched like a motherfucker and was almost black. Fuck balance. It was all a lie.

"Mr. Deadly, sir?"

"Stop calling me sir." Evan ground his teeth. "Leave. I'll take care of myself."

"But, you guys saved my friend once," the older kid said. "After the bombing. She... she was stuck under a wall and you... you got her out. She can help you. She's a doctor. She helps everyone. C'mon, Mr. Deadly, sir. You need to get up." The boy's little hands grasped onto Evan's big arms and yanked but to no avail. "Mason, call an ambulance."

"No," Evan tried to say, but it came out a grunt. He didn't need the hospital, just few minutes and his special body would take care of the rest. If only he could tell them that, but the boy already sounded further away. Evan was slipping, head swimming, walls fading. Tiny footsteps echoed. A siren wailed. The alley blurred, becoming as black as his temper, and everything faded.

TWO

DR. GRACE GO

"EXTRA! *Extra! Two years since Cardinal Bombing! New leads could find perpetrators.*"

Grace Go stopped in her tracks as the newspaper boy's powerful voice carried across the busy sidewalk and bustling morning crowd. Someone bumped into her from behind and cursed at her. She cast a hasty apology over her shoulder and forced her feet to move out of the crushing horde's way. Being an emergency physician gave her exceptional acting skills and emotional control. The trick was to detach yourself from the world. Disconnect from the emotion of the trauma. Spend your life busy and avoid focusing on your own miseries. Like the letter she crumpled into her bag and its headline, written in bold: *Notice of Case Closure.*

She had fourteen days to come up with the goods on the bombing that killed her parents, and forty-nine other innocent souls. It was the only way she'd get justice for the people left homeless and destitute and maybe, just maybe, she'd be able to put her parents to rest.

A twisted feeling churned in her stomach as the words *new leads* bounced around her head. She closed her eyes to center herself and shivered. A brisk rub of her scarred forearms barely warmed her, because the coldness in the pit of her stomach wasn't elemental, it was guilt. She'd survived. Her parents had died. It should never have happened.

Another bump on the shoulder as someone rushed past.

"Sorry," she said without looking up, and clutched her bag tight.

Street sounds amplified. Tires roared on the wet street, and the heavy footsteps of human traffic became a stampede. The repetitive clinking of loose change in a homeless man's cup rattled her spine. Her head felt light. Dizzy. Must be low blood pressure. She'd had only four hours sleep last night, too busy scouring the internet for the identity of the mystery woman she'd seen at the bombing, but she did that every night. Why would it matter today?

Because it's been two years, dummy. Two years since her parents got sick of coming second to her crazy work hours. Two years since they decided to buy an apartment close to her own. Two years since she'd heard her father's guffaw of a laugh, and her mother's sweet, soft voice. Grace squeezed the tears from her eyes and resolved to deal with the pain like every other time. Squash it deep down and keep busy.

An arctic breeze wafted the paperboy's voice back across the street again. "... *New leads bring us...*"

Her heart stopped—new leads—and started beating again. Remembering what it was that halted her the first time, her foot left the sidewalk to cross, but a horn blared a warning and she jumped backwards with a gasp, narrowly missing the fender of a pickup truck as it tore down the street. Water sprayed onto the path, bathing her black jeans in cold.

A man cursed out the window and flipped her the bird, his voice quickly swallowed by the cacophony of city life once again.

Grace tried again. This time, she checked carefully both ways, then rushed to the other side where the grubby newsboy smiled back at her as she drew near. He stood next to a stack of folded papers and an upturned baseball cap for money.

"Hey Taco." Grace smiled and held up a coin.

Taco grinned and handed her a folded newspaper. "Hey Miss. Grace. Boy am I glad to see you."

"I always love seeing you, Taco." The cold pit in her stomach returned when she remembered the letter in her bag. It would affect Taco and his younger brother. She scanned the front page of the newspaper. "New leads, huh?"

He shrugged, unconcerned as only a child would be. "Wasn't them."

Then Taco gave her shifty eyes and checked over his

shoulder. His mouth opened like he wanted to say something, but there were too many people around and he shut it again.

Odd, Grace thought. She hoped he was okay. She'd had a soft spot for Taco and his younger brother since the bombing. Most of their family perished in the explosion except for a single aunt who was pulled from the wreckage, much like Grace. Grace had found them an apartment in her own building, but even being rent controlled, it was hard for the woman to manage. Better to stay a minute and see if Taco was okay.

"I agree. It can't be them. I don't think they've been sighted around town for months. Probably given up or gone missing," Grace elaborated.

"Nah... just waiting."

"For what?"

"Someone to believe in them."

"Yeah, I know, buddy," she said with a sigh, and resisted the urge to ruffle his hair. It was flattened on the top, most likely from the cap he'd removed to collect payment. "It would be nice to have something to believe in, wouldn't it?"

"I mean it, Grace. They didn't do it."

"You're preaching to the choir." She'd been touting the same words since the bombing. During the first month the police had humored her and listened to her wild stories. She'd told anyone and everyone about the strange people she saw dressed in white robes and masks. Except, the

CCTV footage showed only the Deadly Seven lurking suspiciously before the bomb went off. Looking back now, no wonder they thought she suffered post-traumatic stress. The things she saw sounded crazy. She still had trouble organizing the events in her head. Better to avoid the subject in public, and tackle it at home because either someone doctored the video footage, or she really was insane.

"You watch the game last night, Taco?"

"Sure did. We won!"

"Didn't Cardinal City lose?"

"Nah, nobody goes for Cardinal these days. They're at the bottom of the ladder. Miss. Grace..." Taco hushed his tone and ushered her closer. "I *really* need to tell you something."

The poor boy was busting to tell her something. It looked like he needed to pee.

Grace dipped her head, close enough to hear the wheeze in Taco's lungs as he took a breath. Sounded congested. Way too much fluid in there.

"We found someone in the alley this morning," Taco said. "Took him to the hospital for you. And get this, he was... well. You need to talk to him."

Grace's brows lifted. Another homeless person for her to rescue? While her heart warmed at the altruistic innocence of those boys, they flirted with danger. "Have you been out before sunrise again? You know the neighborhood's not safe, Taco."

"It wasn't too early."

"Taco!" Grace shook him gently by the shoulders. "It's dangerous. Do you hear me? Never go out at night again. *Promise me.*" The desperation made her voice tight. The things she'd seen in Emergency on night shift still gave her nightmares. The streets were filled with stupid and violent people, they were certainly no place for children.

"Okay, okay."

"Say it."

"Fine. We won't go out at dark again."

"Even for a few minutes before the sun comes up."

"Yeah, okay." Taco coughed.

"Good. And that wheeze doesn't sound good. How long have you had that?"

"Yeah but—"

A shadow smashed past the two of them at an alarming speed, scooping up Grace's bag, tugging it roughly from her shoulder. She almost lost her arm as the bag tore free. The cry of surprise barely left her lips before the crowd swallowed the thief again.

"Damn it!" Grace desperately tracked the path the thief had gone.

"You want me to chase him Miss. Grace?" Taco's words caught on some phlegm and he coughed into his fingerless gloved hands.

She shook off the irritation of having her bag stolen. No use chasing him down. He was too fast, and she was already late. Muggings were a dime a dozen in Cardinal

City, hence why she never carried valuables. "No, that's okay. There wasn't much in the bag, anyway. You've got work to do and, besides, like I said, that cough doesn't sound good. Come and see me at the clinic tomorrow, okay? Promise? I'd better go."

Grace gave a hasty wave and then plunged back into the horde, barely hearing Taco's protest. She had to stop encouraging his self-proclaimed mission to clean up the streets. Cardinal City was a lost cause.

Big rain drops started to fall, and she flicked out her newspaper to shield herself, rushing until she arrived at the hospital a few blocks away.

By the time she walked through the emergency entrance, she'd mentally catalogued the items she'd lost in her bag. She rarely brought her wallet to work because she had an account at the cafeteria. Only her phone was in the bag and it was a cheap burner she'd picked up recently when her old cell had died.

That left the letter.

Grace pushed through the emergency entrance and into the waiting room with her game face on. Her heart wrenched at the sound of babies crying, people coughing and groaning. As heartbreaking as it sounded in there, the free clinic was worse, and the reason she worked there two days a week. Those poor people needed medical assistance, and the busy environment was music to her empty soul. When she went through the triage bay door, she paused to gather herself. Hospital smells assaulted her nose: disinfectant; plastic; bleach. It all infused her lungs with an odd sense of rightness. This was where she belonged.

This was who she was.

And she was good at her job.

Grace moved into the secure area and passed the exam bays. All beds were full, and all curtains were drawn. A man laid on a gurney in the hallway, sleeping on his side. He looked stable, so Grace assumed he was where he was meant to be for the moment.

A curtain to Grace's right opened and closed, and Doctor Raseem Patel stepped out. Grace and Raseem interned together years ago but lost contact when she deferred from surgery after the bombing. He wore scrubs, a beaded necklace, and his long dark hair was tied back into a bun at his nape. Despite being a modern, young and hip doctor (his words, not Grace's), Raseem took his job at the hospital seriously, and followed the rules to a T.

"What on earth are you doing here, Grace?" Raseem's thick dark brows rose. "Don't get me wrong, I'm glad you're here but... aren't you a few hours early? I just checked the roster."

Grace bit her lip. Out of everyone, he'd probably send her home. "I know. Thought I could be some help."

"We'll always need help, especially in the ER, but... walk with me." His tone sounded ominous.

Grace followed him to the rotation board where he stood staring, hands on hips.

A yellow square with an affirmation in Grace's handwriting was stuck next to each of the surgeon's names. She had a habit of randomly placing them around the place. Someone had to lift morale, and it may as well be her. The nurses were tired, and the surgeons were exhausted. She should know, she was one once.

Envy ate nothing but its own heart, and she knew that better than anyone. It was all she thought of when she recovered from the bombing that had taken her parents' lives. Her anxiety reared its head too much, and she was fearful of having an attack in the operating theater, so opted to stay out. It was either give in to the guilt and self-loathing, or put it to use. So rather than pine over who she used to be, she put her efforts towards making others feel better.

The Post-it notes were an idea she'd taken from her mother, the high school teacher. *A moment of kindness from you could mean the world to someone else.*

"Is everything okay, Raseem?" Did he hate the notes? Were they too intrusive?

"Well, it's like this." He shot her a sidelong glance. "You remember how we did that emergency appendectomy together in our first year on rotation?"

"How could I forget? The guy had a pericardial tamponade. Completely out of left field considering what he was in for. I still can't believe we saved him."

"Right. But you get what I mean."

"Ugh." Was there a question?

Grace paused and inspected the man. Often people

spoke without words, and sometimes you had to look harder because the truth was crippling. His lips were pinched around the sides, and his pupils were dilated. She caught the twitch of his fingers at the side. He was definitely agitated about something. She cast her mind back to the appendectomy surgery. It had been hours long, and almost a disaster on many fronts. Not only did the patient almost bleed out on the table, but in closing, an exhausted Raseem had fumbled with the stitches, and Grace took over before anyone could notice.

Grace squeezed the man's arm. "Don't worry, Raseem. Your technique is second to none. Even the interns gossip about how great it is. You got this, buddy."

He gave her a soft smile and rubbed the back of his neck. "I'm being stupid."

"Nope. You're not." She was the one afraid to get back into an operating theater. "Sometimes the unexpected happens. Getting anxious before an unfamiliar case is normal."

"You never did."

She swallowed and looked away.

"Sorry," he added. "I know you haven't operated in a while."

"And you're in there every day. You're going to ace it. Do what I used to do. Say something funny to break the ice."

"Yeah, that's a good idea," he mumbled absently. "A joke."

"Do you know what else is a good idea? Letting me clock on early."

"Don't you have anything better to do?"

Grace pretended she didn't hear the tone of pity in Raseem's voice and shook her head.

"Okay then. If you really want to, I guess they do need the extra hand in there. I'll see if someone can handover. It's been a wild night. Meet me here in five."

Yes. She mentally fist pumped. For a minute she thought he would tell her to go home or tell the Chief of Staff. Grace went to the staff locker room and pulled on a fresh pair of green scrubs. When she returned, Raseem waited for her with the ER schedule open on his iPad.

"They're all a bit busy, so I said I'd show you," he said.

"So, busy night, huh?" Graced asked.

"Busy and mad. You know how it is. I know the city has gone downhill since those vigilante cowboys disappeared but, honestly, sometimes I wonder if they feed people crack in the tap water for this amount of crazy to turn up in one night. We've had a few gangland stabbings, bullet wounds, another stuck a cucumber up his anus, and then there's the special one," he said.

"The cucumber wasn't special enough?" Grace laughed.

Raseem handed her the iPad and brought up a patient file. "I consulted briefly on this one. Puncture wound is cleaned and stitched by a nurse. You might want to check the suture work. We suspected internal bleeding, maybe some broken ribs. Bruises over his body. Diagnostic scan reports are just in. I haven't seen them yet."

"Why is he so special?"

Raseem gave her a wry look. "Probably high. Didn't want to relinquish his bag of clothes, fought with the attendants when he was brought in, bit of an A-hole... take your pick."

"Is he dangerous?"

"If we hadn't dosed him, maybe. He's a big man. Just check the scans then bump him out unless he needs surgery for the internal bleeding, then call me. He's in the observation unit."

Raseem handed her the iPad, gave her a lip twitch of gratitude, then walked away.

She checked the scan report and her jaw nearly dropped to the floor. Wow. Just wow. Raseem would be sorry he handed this one over.

THREE

EVAN LAZARUS

FROM THE CORNER of his eye, Evan watched his mother pace beside his hospital bed. Preferring to fixate on the scrap paper in front of him, he ignored her muttered obscenities and traced the lines of the portrait he scribbled with the HB pencil he'd found on the floor.

"I mean, it's not like I didn't prepare you for this," Mary Lazarus said, stopping to glare at him in the way only a parent could. "It's not like you didn't spend your entire life training to avoid this very thing." She punctuated her last words by hitting her palm on the bed.

"Exactly. I'm big and ugly enough to take care of myself. How did you know I was here, anyway?"

She ignored his question and continued with her lecture. "A mother will always be worried about her children, no matter how big and strong they've grown. I gave you the tools to be what this city needs, what this world needs, but ultimately it has to be up to you. Your sin doesn't control you. You control it. Evan. Are you listening?"

"Yes."

"I encouraged you when you chose to slip out into the night and fight crime. I supported you when you chose to pack it all in. But, Evan"—she made a pointed look at his faded bruised face and arms—"I won't stand by idly while you punish yourself for something that's not your fault."

Evan stopped the sweeping line of his pencil stroke and lifted his gaze to focus on her.

The woman stood at five-five but had a deceptively powerful body you wouldn't expect to see on a fifty-year-old woman. Sheathed in black workout attire, she looked fresh and fit. Her dark, silver-streaked long hair had been pulled into a convenient bun at the base of her neck. There were tiny worry lines around her eyes and in between her brows, but if he saw her on the street and had to guess her age, he'd say early forties. You'd hardly know beneath her slick surface laid an ex-assassin of the Hildegard Sisterhood and a sleeping dragon capable of killing the instant it woke. And she'd taught him everything she knew.

"My visions don't predict everything, Evan. I'd much rather you return home where you belong. What's this?" Mary's eyes snagged on something. She caught Evan's wrist in her strong vice-like grip and turned the inner flesh toward her eyes, displaying his Yin-Yang tattoo. Each of his siblings had one, but Evan had embellished his with black geometric and organic patterns that traveled up the natural lines and veins of his body, turning his arm into a work of art reminiscent of his paintings. His eldest brother, Parker, had infused the tattoo ink with an acid based indicator that reacted to each of their individual sins. The more envy registered in Evan's body, the darker his tattoo. It was almost black.

Mary sighed and dropped her forehead to his wrist. She inhaled a shuddering breath, gathering herself. The sight broke Evan's heart. She was disappointed, he knew, but he couldn't help himself. The urges were too strong. Envy had driven him to fight in the underground ring. When they wanted him to fail, it urged him to win. Now he sensed envy in the hospital. In *every* bed. In *every* room. Sick people wanted to be someone else. Staff wanted to be somewhere else. Everyone wanted something they didn't have. Including him.

He tugged his wrist from his mother and scribbled madly on the portrait.

"We should just go," Evan stated, shifting to get out of the bed. "The longer we stay, the more likely they'll discover things they shouldn't about me."

She pushed him back down. "Absolutely not. Your sudden absence will raise more red flags than not. Besides, I've seen the outcome. It's best we stay."

Mary's supernatural visions were what led her to rescue him and his siblings from the lab that created them. Those visions kept them safe from the Sisterhood she betrayed, and the mysterious Syndicate who bank rolled their experiment.

Evan resisted, and she responded with more force. "You may be ten times bigger than me, Evan, but I can drop you like a fly."

He eased off. She was right.

Large brown eyes looked down at him over a straight, no-nonsense nose. Evan supposed he and his siblings didn't look so different from her. It was easy to mistake them as relatives. Evan's biological mother was Caucasian—pale and dark-haired. Mary had been born in Mexico, had olive skin and dark eyes. Her husband Flint, their father figure, was Caucasian too, rounding out the perfect appearances for their family brood.

"I brought spare clothes for you to dress in. Lord knows you can't wear the battle gear home."

"I wore it last night. Nobody seemed to care. In fact, they cheered louder when I took a hit."

"La Hostia." Mary pulled out the gold crucifix from her top and kissed it.

"Since when did you find religion? You didn't even pray when you were a fake nun back in the day."

"I'm not praying now. I'm cursing. And maybe it's because none of you children listen to me."

"Okay, okay. Sorry. What else did you see?" Evan asked, scratching the tattoo on his wrist. "What's got that gleam in your eye?"

Mary toyed with the zip on her jacket. The smile

dancing on her lips was almost undetectable before she squashed it down, letting the hardness take back her features.

"I'm relieved to see you're alive, that's all." She tapped on his drawing. "You need to stop this business about Sara. Focus on finding your own woman. Evan. Look at me."

He did.

"It's not healthy to pine after your brother's dead fiancé."

The pencil snapped in Evan's fingers.

"You know there's another reason for this..." he waved at the paper, unable to come up with the right word.

"Obsession?"

"Investigation! I thought you of all people would understand the dreams. I don't pick them, they pick me."

Mary opened her mouth to say something, then shut it. There was nothing else to say. Hadn't been for two years. He couldn't prove it. *They* couldn't prove it. As far as everyone else knew, Sara had died a martyr in the explosion that ended life as he knew it. But Evan knew. He'd always known.

Sara had been filled to the brim with deadly levels of envy. She wasn't as innocent as she seemed, and when he'd told his family after the fact, they blamed him. Some said he lied, others accused him of making a mistake or taking too long to tell them, and then there was the kicker from Wyatt—*You're just jealous I had someone who loved me.*

They were supposed to support each other as a family,

but the truth was, since Sara had entered their lives years ago, they'd never been the same.

"Whatever," Evan said and scrunched up the drawing. "Maybe you're right. She's dead. It's over. You would have seen a vision otherwise. My dreams aren't the same thing as yours. I'll never be as good."

Mary sighed and searched his eyes with hers. "Look, I'm not saying you're wrong, Evan. I'm not all-seeing. Far from it, in fact. The older I get, the less my gift seems to work, and yours... it's something new. It's bio-engineered. Mutating animal DNA mixed with human. It's one of a kind and we're learning as we go. But, what I am saying is, you need to focus on yourself, on finding the one who will be your perfect balance. From what Gloria said about your condition, I don't believe your dreams are the ability she spoke of. It might be a side-effect, but not the one that should manifest when you meet your perfect balance."

Evan rolled his eyes. "Not this again."

"Yes, this again. I've always believed you would be the first, Evan. You will show them all the way. You're the youngest, you've been exposed to your sin the least. Despite what they all think, Sara wasn't the *one* for Wyatt. He would've felt a noticeable biological response. Gloria programed your DNA that way. Wyatt didn't develop any special abilities, so Sara couldn't have been his match. Simple as that. Everyone needs to forget her and move on."

Mary's faith in him kept Evan from an early grave. But he shook his head, staring down at the crumpled paper in his hand. The idea of there being one person out there for him was too hard to comprehend. "It's all bullshit. My birth mother told you bullshit."

"Watch your language."

"Sorry. But it's true. She was a genius geneticist but she was grade-A crazy. Mad scientist doesn't even begin to describe her drivel."

"Have a little respect for the woman who gave her life for your freedom."

"I shouldn't have brought it up." Evan resisted the urge to say she was the one who'd enslaved them in the first place. Instead, he finished scrunching the portrait into a tight ball and threw it at the curtain surrounding his bed just as it parted on the rails with a fast, metallic whoosh.

The ball bounced off the head of a young brunette woman dressed in green scrubs.

"Oh, good aim," she said, patting her head.

All at once, every hair on Evan's body stood to attention.

Three words, and she held him captive. He could do little else but stare.

Babe. Hot. One word impressions flashed through his mind.

Fascinating. A sprinkle of freckles covered the tip of her button nose. A fine white scar feathered up her chin to her rosy pink lips.

Lick. He had the irrational urge to lick his way up it.

Want.

What the?

He blinked madly as his body reacted uncontrollably. Heat flared up his neck, hitting his cheeks. Pin pricks of sweat tickled his skin as it flamed. He was a long way from being a school boy, so when the telltale tightness grew in his groin, he rushed to cover himself with the sheet.

Shit. What the fuck was wrong with him?

Biological reaction.

The woman bent to pick up the crumpled paper and straightened. When her whiskey brown eyes met his, there was an inexplicable moment of intimacy, of human connection. The world around him fell away, and he felt nothing, no envy, no self-disparagement. It was him and her and the strange notion that she saw through it all. The moment lasted long enough to make his heart thud once... twice in his chest, and then it was gone.

She lifted the paper ball in her hands. "Is this important?"

He shook his head like a dumb-ass.

"He's an artist," Mary said with a pointed look at the paper. "He's very talented."

Evan cleared his throat and glared at his mother, but she didn't seem to mind.

"He has an exhibition in a few nights—"

"Mamà," Evan warned.

"He's also a tattooist. Has his own studio."

Christ. He scrubbed his face, letting his hand drag down over his stubble. He caught a whiff of his body odor and flinched. God, he must look awful. He wanted to crawl under a rock or, better yet, sink beneath the floor and never come out.

Mary kept talking about him. Stop. Please, God, stop embarrassing him. He ground his teeth. "*Mary.*"

"Right." Understanding entered Mary's eyes as she ping-ponged between him and the doctor, then she gathered her things, including the plastic bag holding his Envy fighting leathers. "Right. I'll get out of here and let you do your job, doctor. You'll be wanting some privacy. I'll go and get a coffee. I'll wait for you outside, Evan."

With a secretive smirk, Mary opened the curtain to exit, and then closed it behind her, tugging the width tight to the edge, ensuring maximum privacy.

The last sense of envy in the tiny space vacated. Evan turned his gaze back to the doctor in surprise, realizing only then why he hadn't sensed her approach. She held no envy. None.

NEED TO TALK TO OTHER READERS?

Join Lana's Angels Facebook Group for fun chats, giveaways, and exclusive content. https://www.facebook. com/groups/lanasangels

ALSO BY LANA PECHERCZYK

The Deadly Seven

(*Paranormal Romance*)

The Deadly Seven Box Set Books 1-3

Sinner

Envy

Greed

Wrath

Sloth

Gluttony

Lust

Pride

Despair

Fae Guardians

(*Fantasy/Paranormal Romance*)

Season of the Wolf Trilogy

The Longing of Lone Wolves

The Solace of Sharp Claws

Of Kisses & Wishes Novella (free for subscribers)

The Dreams of Broken Kings

Season of the Vampire Trilogy

The Secrets in Shadow and Blood

A Labyrinth of Fangs and Thorns

Game of Gods

(Romantic Urban Fantasy)

Soul Thing

The Devil Inside

Playing God

Game Over

Game of Gods Box Set

ABOUT THE AUTHOR

OMG! How do you say my name?

Lana (straight forward enough - Lah-nah) **Pecherczyk** (this is where it gets tricky - Pe-her-chick).

I've been called Lana Price-Check, Lana Pera-Chick-ywack, Lana Pressed-Chicken, Lana Pech...*that girl!* You name it, they said it. So if it's so hard to spell, why on earth would I use this name instead of an easy pen name?

To put it simply, it belonged to my mother. And she was my dream champion.

For most of my life, I've been good at one thing – art. The world around me saw my work, and said I should do more of it, so I did.

But when at the age of eight, I said I wanted to write stories, and even though we were poor, my mother came home with a blank notebook and a pencil saying I should follow my dreams, no matter where they take me for they will make me happy. I wasn't very good at it, but it didn't matter because I had her support and I liked it.

She died when I was thirteen, and left her four daughters orphaned. Suddenly, I had lost my dream champion, I was split from my youngest two sisters and had no one to talk to about the challenge of life.

So, I wrote in secret. I poured my heart out daily to a diary and sometimes imagined that she would listen. At the end of the day, even if she couldn't hear, writing kept that dream alive.

Eventually, after having my own children (two firecrackers in the guise of little boys) and ignoring my inner voice for too long, I decided to lead by example. How could I teach my children to follow their dreams if I wasn't? I became my own dream champion and the rest is history, here I am.

When I'm not writing the next great action-packed romantic novel, or wrangling the rug rats, or rescuing GI Joe from the jaws of my Kelpie, I fight evil by moonlight, win love by daylight and never run from a real fight.

I live in Perth Australia, but I'm up for a chat anytime online. Come and find me.

Subscribe & Follow
subscribe.lanapecherczyk.com
lp@lanapecherczyk.com

facebook.com/lanapecherczykauthor

twitter.com/lana_p_author

instagram.com/lana_p_author

amazon.com/-/e/B00V2TP0HG

bookbub.com/profile/lana-pecherczyk